The following chapters are reprinted by permission from the respective magazines: THEORETICAL KILLINGS (OR HYPOTHETICAL KILLERS AND THE MEN WHO LOVE THEM) in *Quarter After Eight*. LIVING WITH A SPIKE IN YOUR BRAIN, in *Roger*. WILL THE REAL K. NELSON PLEASE STAND UP?, in *Packingtown Review*. IMAGE #8 as EXHIBIT #8: THE PEACH PIT RODEO HALF-TIME SHOW in *Ecotone: Reimagining Place*. UNPUBLISHED LETTER TO THE EDITOR in *Matter*. A VICTIM OF SHOES and MAN WALKING DOG FINDS BODY in A. JUMBO HENRY in *Compass*. A LETTER TO THE BIONIC MAN and APOLOGY TO HENRY AARON in *Post Road*. WOODEN INDIAN and HOW TO NOT TELL A STORY ABOUT BLOOD IN A BATHTUB in *Quarterly West*. SMASHING CHAIRS in *Salt Hill*. FIRST STRIKE MONTAGE in *Interim*. Parts of this book also appeared in different forms with different functions in *The Guinness Book of Me: a Memoir of Record*, published in 2005 by Simon & Schuster.

Printed in the United States of America

Library of Congress Control Number: 2009927358

Church, Steven

Theoretical Killings: Essays and Accidents

ISBN: 0-9706190-6-5

ISBN 13: 978-0-9706190-6-8

University of New Orleans Press
unopress.uno.edu

Author's Note

This book is a collection of prose— most of it published previously in literary journals, sometimes in different forms— and it contains overlapping elements of fiction and nonfiction. If the co-habitation of genres bothers the reader, I ask you to accept the following statements as true: I have never had a steel spike lodged in my brain. My father did not hang himself in the garage or collect cane chairs; nor did he work in a factory after the divorce; nor did I witness a girl hurting herself at the Dodge City rodeo where the monkey rode the sheep dog. I am not one of the Holnam Sisters working for the Captain, or an employee of Jumbo Henry, Inc. These things did not happen. They are not true. Everything else then— even if it contains fictional elements— is what I would consider an essay.

PRACTICAL CONCERNS

ഹ ETHICS ൃ

Practical Real-Life Responses to Theoretical Killings
Or Hypothetical Killers & the Men Who Love Them 15

Man Walking Dog Finds Body in Alley 53

Unpublished Letter to the Editor from Mary
Eldest of the Holnam Sisters 57

Apology to Henry Aaron 65

Will the Real K. Nelson Please Stand Up? 71

A Victim of Shoes 115

Exciting New Product Announcements from
Jumbo Henry, Inc. 121

ഹ AESTHETICS ൃ

Living With a Spike in Your Brain 129

How Not to Tell a Story About Blood in a Bathtub:
An Essay on Form 137

Cowboys & Indian Dodge City, 1976 145

The Peach Pit Rodeo Half-Time Show 151

Dear Abe 155

A Letter to the Bionic Man 161

Smashing Chairs: A Refrain 167

Postcards from the Cold War:
Notes on Viewing The Day After, 1983 175

For Sophia, our dancing star.

THEORETICAL
KILLINGS

"One must have chaos within oneself to give birth to a dancing star."

-Friedrich Nietzsche

ETHICS

PRACTICTAL REAL-LIFE RESPONSES TO

THEORETICAL

KILLINGS OR

HYPOTHETICAL KILLERS

&

THE MEN WHO LOVE THEM

Moreover there is one very important element of good in what is here insisted. In real life it would hardly ever be certain that the man on the narrow track would be killed.

The driver of the tram does not then leap off and brain him with a crowbar.

—Philippa Foot[1]

Sometimes, Philippa, we think we're your man on the narrow track waiting to be brained. Sometimes we're the driver, and we've already got the crowbar swinging teeth. Sometimes we're the surgeon; we're Smith and we're Jones. We always take the hook to the skull. You've cleaved us open now.

In the midst of Consequentialism, Kantian Deontology, we cling to the roots of narrative. Runaway trolleys, rogue doctors, killing

---

[1] "The Problem of Abortion and the Doctrine of Double Effect." *Oxford Review* (1967). Ms. Foot seems to be referring to the case of the State of California vs. Everly, wherein a Mr. Bernard Everly, Tram Driver, did in fact leap from the tram, brain a passerby with a crowbar, and throw him under the wheels in an effort to stop a runaway tram.

machines, poisoned gas, drowning children, crushed children, starving children, fat men in caves, fat men on trolley tracks, swamped rowboats, lifeboats— like this whole hidden sub-genre of pulp fiction with characters named John and Mary; named X and Y, A and B; named Smith, poor misguided Smith and the sad Fat Man. The theoretical crushing of children, that's what we're talking about.

This is all we can do. Runaway trolleys rattle through our brains. We're glutton-fish for the stories[2]. Tell us more. Tell us we're good.

---

[2] Here's one: *But now let me ask you to imagine this. You wake up in the morning and find yourself back to back in bed with an unconscious violinist. He has been found to have a fatal kidney ailment, and the Society of Music Lovers has canvassed all the available medical records and found that you alone have the right blood type to help. They have therefore kidnapped you, and last night the violinist's circulatory system was plugged into yours, so that your kidneys can be used to extract poisons from his blood as well as your own... the violinist is plugged into you. To unplug you would be to kill him. But never mind, it's only for nine months...All persons have a right to life, and violinists are persons. Granted you have a right to decide what happens in and to your body, but a person's right to life outweighs your right to decide what happens in and to your body. So you cannot ever be unplugged from him.* From Judith Jarvis Thomson, "A Defense of Abortion," *Philosophy & Public Affairs*, 1/1 (Fall, 1971), 47-66.

HERE IS THE HOOK:

Innocent Bystander *strolling by the trolley track*. Driver slumped over the wheel, flat dome of his head pressed up against the glass. Five workmen on the main track. A sidetrack! A switch there, sticking out of the pavement like Excalibur— that infamous sword of destiny. But... one workman on the sidetrack. *What to do?* You have been chosen... *He stamped on the brakes, the brakes failed, so he fainted. Well, here is the switch, which you can throw, thereby turning the trolley yourself. Of course you will kill one if you do. What to do?*

Judith Jarvis Thomson[3]

---

[3] Thomson, Judith Jarvis. "The Trolley Problem." *Rights, Restitution and Risk: Essays on Moral Philosophy.* Ed. William Parent. Cambridge, MA: Harvard University Press, 1986. Critics have panned Ms. Thomson's flippant, casual tone when discussing such morbid and painful events. Her jaunty, "Well, here is . . ." and her equally dismissive "What to do?" conjure up a dilemma more akin to the choice of whether to kill a fly or shoo it out the door, rather than the question of when it is morally permissible to harm some in order to save others.

THE CHOICE: A THREE ACT PLAY

Act 1:

Scene: Trolley Track. Fluttering birds. Thunderous noise. Chaos as the trolley approaches, rattling wheels echo in the theater, screams layered in for effect. Spotlight on you. You're alone with your decision and your antagonist, Moral Intuition. A decision must be made. Drama. Tension. Suspense. The stuff of narrative. We begin in media res.

MORAL INTUITION: Kill the one workman.

YOU: Really?

MI: Obviously.

YOU: Are you sure?

MI: Yes. What other choice do you have?

YOU: But...

MI: Trust me.

Dear Judith Jarvis Thomson,

Why is it that so many of you academics have three names? My name isn't fancy, just Harold "Smitty" Smith. I work track maintenance for the San Francisco Trolley Authority. Friends call me "Smitty." I'm writing because of that article you published about the runaway trolley and the transplant surgeon. Though I appreciate your drawing attention to the dangers of trolley work, I feel the need to take issue with some of the factual presentation of your stories.

Now I understand that you may not have had the opportunity to properly research the mechanics of trolley operation but you have to be careful with the things you say. I mean, think about it. It just doesn't happen the way you say it happens. First of all, we don't have runaway trolleys. It just doesn't happen. Ever.

Second. We don't give any old bum walking down the street access to track switches. Think of the chaos. Is that what you want? Even when the switches were manually operated, the switchman was a highly trained individual. He had to take classes and he carried a lot of important keys.

Of course now it's all computerized. You have to have letters after your name to run it now. Fucking administrators now with their degrees and shit... My father, he worked for the SFTA. Fifty years. Never finished high school. And I remember this old switchman who used to drink bourbon with my father after work. He had a voice like burlap and these eyes I swear could look right through all the flesh and bone of your body, right at the wink of your soul. He carried this big silver ring full of keys on his belt. He jingled when he walked. That's all I remember. He jingled and I wanted it.

Now nobody expects the average bystander to assume responsibility for anyone's life but his or her own. Not anymore, much less the lives of five strangers. You know what I mean? Take me. I've been working for the Authority for twenty years and they won't let me anywhere near the rooms where they control the traffic, the big rooms downtown with padded chairs. And you might think this would grind on me, wear me down to a little nub of a man.

You might think I could show up at the maintenance garage one morning with a pistol, that I might shoot five of my coworkers (maybe two managers) and then turn the gun on myself.... And I might, but I probably won't. I'm much more innocent, much subtler than this. I work behind the scenes. Besides, trouble just has this way of nipping at my heels. It's always there, setting these traps for me to stumble into... But that's not my point here. I'm digressing. I do that sometimes.

What I want to stress is the importance of facts. The truth matters. You can't just say things like "all things being equal" and have all things be equal. It doesn't work that way in life. I mean, the stuff you talk about isn't real. It can't actually happen. I know this. And you can't change that. Really, I suggest you do some further research in the future. Please feel free to call me if you have questions about the mechanics of trolley track operations. Don't bother with the suits at Central Ops. They're all idiots anyway. Thanks for your time.

Best,

Harold "Smitty" Smith

It's true. These stories speak to you, the reader. Directly. That "you" pronoun necessarily implicates us, the reader, the participant, the innocent bystander. It demands of us our attention, our decision-making abilities. It asks us to participate as a character. There is tension; there is conflict between the healthy and the sick, the agents and the innocents. Movement. Arc. Dénouement. And resolution. We eat it up. And we especially like surprises— the odd machinations of philosopher's minds, the details of death and killing, and the absurd situational drama. Row boats. Caves. Unconscious violinists. Runaway trolleys. Everything bad happens in theoretical time. Everything bad happens to someone else. All things being equal...

...This time you are to imagine yourself to be a surgeon, a truly great surgeon. Among other things you do, you transplant organs, and you are such a great surgeon that the organs you transplant always take. At the moment, you have five patients who need organs. Two need one lung each, two need a kidney each, and the fifth needs a heart. If they do not get these organs today, they will all die...

But where to find the lungs, kidneys, and the heart?

The time is almost up when a report comes... a young man who has just come into your clinic for his yearly check-up has exactly the right blood-type, and is in excellent health.

Lo, you have a possible donor.

All you need to do is cut him up and distribute his parts among the five who need them. You ask, but he says, "Sorry, I deeply sympathize, but no." Would it be morally permissible for you to operate anyway?

Judith Jarvis Thomson

THE CHOICE: A THREE ACT PLAY

Act 2

Scene: Surgeon's office. Mysterious beeping. Vivaldi in the background. The anonymous whir of hospital noise. Almost peaceful. Lots of white. Spotlight on you, Mr. Surgeon. You're alone with a decision and antagonist, Moral Intuition. A decision must be made. Five will die. You can save them. Drama. Tension. Suspense. The stuff of narrative. We begin in media res.

MORAL INTUITION: Let the five die.

YOU: Really?

MI: Obviously.

YOU: Are you sure?

MI: Yes. What other choice do you have?

YOU: But...

MI: Trust me.

YOU: But I can't.

MI: Why not?

UPSHOT: If we are to trust your Moral Intuition, this is what the Surgeon must do: The Surgeon (S) must kill that one healthy innocent patient (Z) and must do it quickly, perhaps under the ruse of a routine blood draw or just a quick plunge of a needle into Z's thigh, a huge dose of morphine or something stronger to knock him out there on the exam table before S can stop his heart for good. The Surgeon might want to bring that big orderly, Tito and JC the nurse— a couple of big guys in case things get weird. S may want to bring some leather straps. Just in case. S might want to keep him alive for a while but buried in a drug-induced coma until everyone is ready. Make sure your nurse, Karen, gets everyone ready. Make sure there are no mistakes. S doesn't want to do this again. S is not going to find a better subject than this one. Z is a big kid, strong and vital, the perfect sort of patient for what you have to do. He looks like a person who is loved. Someone has ironed his shirt. His shoes are new. He probably eats well, doesn't smoke, and works out. But S cannot think too much about these things because there is a role to play, a job to do in this corresponding dilemma. S has five lives to save and no time can be wasted. It's a simple thing, really. It's just living up to the Hippocratic Oath to minimize harm. And S is good at this. S is an excellent surgeon, a doctor who has saved many lives. S knows this because they've been counted, the information carefully memorized by S. By some estimates, it's 72 lives saved directly because of S's actions. That's a lot. That means something. He wouldn't forget a thing like that. S is not some rogue doctor harvesting organs to sell on the black market. S is trying to do good in the world, trying to minimize harm and suffering; and we'd like to think that this boy, this Patient Z on the table, would maybe understand this and recognize the dilemma here. Someone has to make the hard decisions, the really hard one. S likes to think this boy, Z might even volunteer himself to save those five strangers because he is just that sort of guy. S doesn't know that, in fact, Z is NOT that kind of guy. That sort of personality quirk isn't in the report he gets. As simple readers and citizens we don't know anything about Z except for his blood-type and his name. We don't know that he has an older brother who works for the city. We don't know that this brother recently made a difficult decision in the face of unimaginable stress and tragedy, a decision in the heat of the moment, a decision very similar to this Surgeon's decision— all things being equal— that in some ways unleashed a chain of events leading up to this moment, here in S's office, on the operating table for Z, the clock tick-ticking in the background, the hum and whir of machinery, and the five dying patients surrounding the Patient like the points of a star. Because that's what S is in this dilemma. S is a star. A rock-star surgeon, the kind of guy they make reality TV shows about because of good looks and skill and because S saves lives. These 5 lives. And S understands the costs of this kind of thinking. The Surgeon understands that Z must die so that others might live.

But why? Why is it OK to kill in one case but not the other? This is the root of our problem. We want to say that somehow killing that one lonely fat workman (probably some guy with raging b.o. and annoying habits that drive the other workmen absolutely bonkers) is worse than letting those five unlucky patients die (patients whose conditions may be nobody's fault but their own). Consequentialist Us, the innocent bystander at the switch, wants to believe that an action is right if and only if it maximizes good consequences. In the Trolley Case, harm is inevitable, and we can minimize that harm (thereby maximizing good consequences) by flipping the switch. But the Consequentialist Agent seems cold and heartless in the Transplant case, seems like some kind of sadistic doctor killing patients for kicks, maybe even for his own mistakes. Consequentialist Agent takes a beating from Kantian Agent, the believer in absolutes, when we're talking about the Surgeon. We just don't like him any longer.

The truth is that, as a reader and a moral agent, we don't care much for the Surgeon's character. Not our kind of guy, not one with whom we can identify, not someone we "care" about in this narrative. We feel the Bystander's pain. We cannot say the same for the Surgeon. His conflict doesn't punch like the Trolley does; and the you in Transplant just alienates the reader. This is the danger of such choices in craft. Point-of-view cannot be taken lightly when we're talking about ethics.

Dear Judith J. Thomson,

My name is Samuel S. Lapchik, and I work as a detective for an obscure governmental agency with a name that sounds something like "artichoke" (but not quite). I am investigating a not-so-recent incident involving a runaway trolley in which five innocent track workmen were tragically killed. I'm hoping you might be able to shed some light on the events. You seem, in many ways, to know more about this than we do, and this is troubling for a variety of reasons— not the least of which being that this is exactly the sort of thing that obscure governmental agencies should know about.

We have one eyewitness— a Chinese street musician who plays "Johnny B. Good" on a toy guitar— and a bystander who was involved in the incident. Both individuals reported seeing a monkey near the switch-box around the time of the incident. However, the eyewitness cannot confirm the presence of a monkey handler; and the Bystander dodged all questions about a monkey. Anecdotal evidence supports my belief that this monkey may have belonged to a Mr. Smith who lived in the neighborhood. I also understand that this same Mr. Smith may have worked for you in the past as an independent contractor. I would appreciate it if you could contact me immediately with any information you might have about Mr. Smith's whereabouts. Thank you for your time.

Sincerely,

Samuel Lapchik

Special Agent

COP-OUT ARGUMENT: The actions of both the Innocent Bystander and the Transplant Surgeon are morally blameworthy.

PREMISE: You must not treat the one workman only as a means to your ends (from the Kantian Categorical Imperative). You, Mr. Bystander, are morally wrong in your actions.

> It should be clear, I think, that "kill" and "let die" are too blunt to be useful tools for the solving of this problem. We ought to be looking within killings and savings for the ways in which the agents would be carrying them out.
>
> —Judith Thomson

Dear Judith calls out: Loop variation: (see diagram: side spur looping back around again to the main track) Now we make him a means. Now you need his body to stop the trolley. But what if he's too thin? What if his slight build, his petite figure, his smallish skull were not enough to jam the rolling wheels, not enough drag to stop the trolley. A skinny man might just come apart like a doll, like he's made of sticks and twine. He might not even slow down the trolley. You need someone not easily rendered into parts. You need someone like an anchor, a drag break, a wedge. You need someone to die.

AND RESPONSE:

Judith now gives us: *Fat Man Variation:*

Let us now imagine that the five on the straight track are thin, but thick enough so that although all five will be killed if the trolley goes straight, the bodies of the five will stop it, and it will therefore not reach the one. On the other hand, the one on the right hand track is fat, so fat that his body will by itself stop the trolley, and the trolley will therefore not reach the five. May the agent turn the trolley?

Judith Jarvis Thomson

"The Trolley Problem"

THE CHOICE: A THREE ACT PLAY

Act 3:

Scene: Bridge over trolley track. Birds chirping. Same noise from Act 1– screaming brakes, thundering wheels. Voices of passengers calling out for help. You approach a hugely fat man standing on the bridge. He wears sweatpants and white socks, black Reeboks, and a T-shirt that advertises some sort of Aquarium or undersea adventure. He's drinking a Slurpee with a long red straw, and he's just hit bottom. Somehow you can hear the raspy sucking sound of it over the noise of the trolley, and this is the last thing you remember of the Fat Man. The sound of his empty cup. Spotlight on you, Mr. Bystander. You're alone with your decision and your antagonist, Moral Intuition. The "switch" is different, but a decision must be made. Five will die. You can save them. Drama. Tension. Suspense. The stuff of narrative. We begin in media res.

MORAL INTUITION: Kill the fat man. Shove his ass right over the handrail. You'll probably need a running start. Dip your shoulder and aim for the small of his back.

YOU: Really?

MI: Obviously. We've been through this already.

YOU: Are you sure?

MI: Yes. What other choice do you have?

YOU: But...

MI: Trust me.

HERE IS WHAT HAPPENS WHEN WE'VE FALLEN IN LOVE WITH THEORETICAL KILLERS:

We hardly leave the house. We pile on pounds of fat and muscle. People begin to notice our goodness. We poke a new hole in the belt with a knife so it will fit our expanding girth. We don't move much. Instead we occupy our heads with the Trolley Problem. We find new stories and storytellers: F.M. Kamm, H.M. Malm, Benditt, Ravizza, Feinberg, Quinn. We find Foot and Thomson, Harris and Rachels. But it is Malm who troubles us most. Her theory is dense, her writing blunt but elusive— almost like Carver, like language poetry, like song. Her essays peppered with stories of John and Mary and the twisted Smith. She keeps our heads busy for months. She makes us hurt. And the hurt is good.

RESPONSE: H.M. MALM

Imagine a machine containing two children, John and Mary. If one pushes a button, John will be killed, but Mary will emerge unharmed. If one does not push the button, John will emerge unharmed, but Mary will be killed.[4]

A railway train whose brakes have just failed is headed down track A. Smith, a bystander, can divert the train onto track B by pulling a nearby lever. If Smith pulls the lever, John, who is tied on track B, will be hit by the train and killed. If Smith does not pull the lever, Mary, who is tied on track A, will be hit by the train and killed.

H.M. Malm [5]

---

[4] "As an example of a case in which death was not (at least) morally random to begin with, suppose that Mary was placed where she is because she is a little girl and whoever set up the machine wanted to kill a little girl, and John was placed where he is because the machine would not function without a counterbalancing weight." Footnote 17, p. 252 (see below)

[5] Malm, H. M.. "Killing, Letting Die, and Simple Conflicts." *Philosophy and Public Affairs* 238 (1989).

Dear Dr. Malm,

I don't know what world raised you to adulthood, what culture taught you your lessons, but I feel compelled to address what I see as a disturbing pattern in your writing toward the repeated abstraction from the graphic horrors of infanticide. I am a mother. That is something. Perhaps you don't know anything about what it's like to give birth, to raise children. You're probably one of those childless academics. Maybe a lesbian. I don't know. I don't know these things about you. I only know what I read. I have two young children, John and Mary. They are the lights of my life— like fireflies in the dark sometimes. And I don't know why you felt the need to put John and Mary into your awful killing machine. Sure, they're just names. But they are the names of MY children. Do you get that? Couldn't you have used Child X and Child Y, or how about no children at all. You could have used monkeys. Perhaps you, like me, have experienced some trauma in your life. Well, let me assure you, dear, that you cannot hide behind hypotheticals. There is no escape in theory. Don't get me wrong. I do respect the academic pursuits. But I just think that if you ever had children of your own, ever saw the look of love in their eyes, you wouldn't be writing those awful things about killing machines and runaway trolleys.

Sincerely,

Bev Knight

Lancaster, PA

Response: H.M. Malm

Smith walks into a room and discovers that a machine that has been set to crush the child inside has malfunctioned. Smith knows that he could restart the machine...and he does so solely because he is curious to see how flat a person can be.

Imagine a machine containing two children, John and Mary.

John and Mary are drowning on opposite sides of a pier. Agent Smith, who cannot swim, is standing on top of the pier and has access to one life preserver.

If Smith does not throw the life preserver at all, both Mary and John will die.[6]

H.M. Malm

---

[6] Ibid.

Truman Capote fell in love with Perry Smith. Cold-blooded killer or not, this much seems obvious. At the very least he inhabited Perry's consciousness for a work of nonfiction. There was some combination of brutality and intelligence; some balance between hard and soft, between truth and fiction, that attracted Capote to this killer of the Clutter family. We've begun to suspect there is something similar in the character Smith we find attractive.[7] If he was locked up in a cell somewhere,

---

[7] The following passage was excerpted from an unprecedented interview conducted with agent Smith, a suspected theoretical killer, while he was awaiting sentencing at the maximum-security prison in Leavenworth, Kansas. I was still recovering from knee surgery and had just begun walking without the movable brace. Inmate Smith was kept in solitary confinement most of the time; and I happened to be his first visitor.

Inmate Smith does not have easy eyes. He sits down at the interview table, his hands chained to a leather belt on his waist and his ankles bound together. He stares hard at me. His fingertips curl up over the top of the table and I notice that his nails are clipped short. He has recently shaved all the hair from his face and his eyebrows are nicked with little cuts. I am admittedly somewhat nervous, and Smith can sense this. Before we can begin, he asks me several times if I'd like a cigarette. Despite the fact that I've never smoked in my life, I pause at his first question— the suggestive power of his voice drawing me closer. *Don't you want a cigarette?* Perhaps it's the fluorescent lights in the room and the silence; but after he asks for the third time, I actually do crave a cigarette. I can almost imagine that initial suck of smoke, that release, and repeat. I pull out my pad of paper and start the tape recorder.

Me: What, if anything, would you like to say to the public, to your victims, before your sentencing?

Smith: You don't waste any time do you?

Me: Well…?

Smith: What victims? You're looking at one right here, buddy.

Me: You seem unrepentant to say the least. Are you capable of expressing any remorse for your actions?

Smith smiles, rolls his eyes, and bobs his head as if he was expecting this question.

S: Well of course your use of the word "capable" nicely loads your question and forces me to defend my "capability" when what you're really asking about is my

we'd visit him, bring him soap and baked goods. We'd ask him all

"willingness" to express remorse.

M: OK.

S: So ask the question again.

M: OK, are you willing to express any remorse for the torture and killing of innocents?

S: Though I might take issue with your use of the word "torture," I will respond by saying that remorse is the emotional response they want. The problem is I'm just diverting harm, just changing the course of things. What the public wants is closure. But closure is a myth, an invention of those who've never lost. And I refuse to make their pleasantly principled grief that much easier.

Smith tries to talk with his hands, but they look a little silly flailing around at his waist, tied just below the edge of the table.

M: But don't you feel as though you owe them something?

S: Once again, it's those little words that trip you up. "Owe" suggests some sort of obligation. But what kind of obligation might this be? What is the nature of this obligation?

M: Well, clearly not a legal obligation. How about moral? That seems pretty obvious.

S: Granted. But that still assumes that I'm operating under some sort of normative code of conduct. If I've shown anything with my actions— and I know you've done your research— it should be that I'm not limited by any ethical code. Think about it. You'd be hard-pressed to show how ethics helps in the situations I was faced with, situations where you have no choice but to act in ways that seem intuitively "wrong."

Smith opens his palms and bends forward, almost as if he is bowing.

M: Let's move on to something else

S: Sure. How about your wife's panties?

M: Let's talk about your background, your childhood. What's your earliest happy memory?

Smith ignores my question. He looks around the small drab interview room.

S: I had a pet monkey.

M: Excuse me?

S: A monkey. A squirrel monkey. He was my best friend.

M: That's nice. Did your parents buy him for you?

S: No, you idiot. I mean before I came here, before all this crap. I had a pet monkey. He lived in my apartment.

M: What's his name.

S: He's probably dead. Can you find out for me? Can you tell me what happened?

M: I can try. What's his name?

S: I bet they killed him.

M: His name?

S: Carl. (I write this down on my pad of paper, "Ask about Carl the monkey.")

M: I'll see what I can do.

S: I loved that monkey.

Smith looks at me and waits for a reaction. I decide to change the subject.

M: How do you spend your free time here, your time alone in your cell?

S: Don't laugh.

M: I won't.

S: I carve sheep from soap. Other animals too. Snowshoe hares, arctic foxes, white rhinos and tigers. I smuggle the bars in from the shower, hide them where I can. Had a little jackknife for a while— but the guards freaked and took it. I use my fingernails to carve or anything else— even my teeth sometimes.

He looks back at the door and leans over the table.

S: (He whispers.) I have one for you. Here, in my pocket. (He gestures toward the pocket with his chin.) Go on. Take it.

I check the door, reach over the table, and pull a tiny white horse from his pocket. Clearly carved from soap, it softens a little in my sweaty fingers. I thank him for the gift and slip it into my shirt pocket. Later I will notice the detail— the flowing mane, nostrils, teeth, and hooves. I will think about his missing monkey.

M: Let's talk about John and Mary.

S: What about them? They're terribly resilient children.

Smith grins at this.

M: Why these children? Some kind of personal vendetta?

S: None of this is personal, my friend. Really, I think you can blame Malm and Rachels for much of this. John and Mary are children after all. They don't know any better. I mean, would you climb into a machine like that? It's the philosophers, the ethicists, who are the real sickos.

M: But how do you explain the apparent series of coincidences that always seems to bring you and these two children together?

A guard raps on the window in the door. He holds his wristwatch up to the

sorts of questions about his earliest happy memories. We'd probably ask about his mother's hands and the name of his first pet.

---

window, points at the face, and says, "Five minutes, Smith."

S: But it's not a coincidence at all, friend. It's all intentional. I am who I am. And those two children play their roles. They are walking talking innocence. If it wasn't John and Mary it would be two other children.

M: But why children? It's just wrong.

S: Exactly. Imagine I had stumbled upon a killing machine containing not children but two journalists. (He winks.) We need their helplessness. Without it, the lessons don't mean as much. I mean, who cares if a journalist gets crushed flat. Who learns anything from that?

Smith laughs and slaps his leg.

S: So why did you come here?

M: It's the stories about you— so graphic, so cold, so heartless? Unbelievable, really. I guess I wanted to get a little closer to the truth.

S: See that's what theory is, fundamentally. Heartless. Necessarily so. This is not an exercise of the heart muscle.

M: Yes, but it's a story. A story— something that necessarily demands some sort of emotional response, some reaction from the reader. It asks you to participate.

S: You expect too much from your stories.

M: Perhaps.

The guard thumps on the door again. "Time's up, Smith." Two large men wearing white rubber gloves enter the room. One of them holds his baton ready. The other opens Smith's shackles, releasing him from the chair. As they are taking him out of the room, Smith looks back at me.

S: Don't come back, OK? I don't need this. (But his eyes are fixed on mine; beaming a plea for help. He raises his nicked-up eyebrows and shows me his teeth.)

When I leave the prison that day, the heat is oppressive— already one hundred degrees with ninety-five percent humidity. As I climb into my car and roll down the windows, I look down at my shirt. The pocket is stained and greasy. I reach inside and pull out Smith's carved gift horse— the fine features beginning to melt already. The horse sticks to my fingers. And before I drive away from the prison, I lift a soapy finger to my mouth and touch it to my tongue... but I have said more than I should. Two weeks later Smith escaped from prison guards who were transporting him to another facility. He was last seen jumping into a green Volvo station wagon with the vanity license plate "SOPHIA." Eyewitness accounts describe the driver as a bearded man wearing a tweed sport coat with leather patches.

After Malm's stories, it's easy to lose yourself in theory, swimming around in the Doctrine of Double Effect, words like "normative" and "optimific," and latch onto the hypothetical situations. You might imagine bombing runs. You are Terror Bomber (TB), Strategic Bomber (SB). You paddle rowboats and steer runaway trolleys. You push fat men off of bridges and use them as means to all my ends. Ethical theory lets me live in this world, lets me tread safely in analytical shoes through these gothic halls. It's a nice walk.

Still, you fill out the back of your driver's license: Everything but the Eyes. Because you like to believe that shit about the eyes being the seat of the soul.

Smith is everywhere, it seems. Just look in the phone book, the newspapers. You hate to say he's in your home, but it's true. He's in your family, too. He's your uncle, your cousin, your neighbor, and the mailman. Everyone is Smith.

ARGUMENT: KILLING IS MORALLY WORSE THAN LETTING DIE[8]
RESPONSE: JAMES RACHELS

In the first, Smith stands to gain a large inheritance if anything should happen to his six-year-old cousin. One evening while the child is taking his bath, Smith sneaks into the bathroom and drowns the child, and then arranges things so that it will look like an accident.

In the second, Jones also stands to gain if anything should happen to his six-year-old cousin. Like Smith, Jones sneaks in planning to drown the child in his bath. However, just as he enters the bathroom Jones sees the child slip and hit his head, and fall face down in the water. Jones is delighted; he stands by, ready to push the child's head back under if it is necessary, but it is not necessary. With only a little thrashing about, the child drowns all by himself, "accidentally", as Jones watches and does nothing.[9]

James Rachels

---

[8] This sounds nice. Easy enough. Intuitively appealing.

[9] Rachels, James. "Active and Passive Euthanasia." *The New England Journal of Medicine* 292 (1975).

Dear Dr. Rachels,

How can you live with yourself? I am a mixed-blood Navajo, and I do not take stories lightly. My father's culture believes in the power of stories, the power of imagination to bring to life. After having read your essay, "Active and Passive Euthanasia," I felt compelled to write you. My father died last year and it still hurts. Perhaps you've received stacks of mail, perhaps only my letter. Perhaps you've thought about this. How can you live with these men in your mind, these killers Smith and Jones? They must take up so much room with their killing ways. They must lurk in the dark corners, in between the lines, and come calling in the night for your soul. You imagined that child thrashing about in the bathtub. You created him with your images and did nothing to save him. I'm not expecting some hero on a white horse, some Superman to save him; but what about justice, redemption, and remorse? What about punishment? I hold you equally responsible for the killing of these innocent children. Their deaths will be smudge marks on your soul.

Sincerely,

Lyle Morgan

Who is worse? Smith or Jones? Who would you hire to babysit your children? It comes back to this question: is there a morally relevant difference between killing and letting die? Does it matter? Is there a morally relevant difference between letting die and killing? Is every killing a kind of letting die, every letting a kind of killing too? Is it permissible for the Bystander to flip the switch and for the Transplant Surgeon to let the five die? Is it permissible to flip that quick? How can we trust such fickle intuitions? The trick is to find an ethical code, a critical theory of conduct that morally permits you— the agent, the reader— to live in the skin of both Bystander and Surgeon, both Smith and Jones.

Dear Dr. Rachels,

My name is Samuel S. Lapchik and I am a detective with an obscure governmental agency with a name that sounds something like "artichoke" (but not quite). I was referred to you by the parents of John and Mary. I am investigating the movements of a suspected serial child-killer, a clearly evil man, who goes by the name of "Smith." Perhaps you've heard of him. What we have here is the question of theodicy.[10] I believe you know whereof I speak. I believe Mr. Smith was (or is still currently) an employee of your designs. Perhaps you're aware that he has also contracted his services to a Mr. Rachels (and perhaps more). Perhaps you're aware that, thanks to this Mr. Rachels, your Mr. Smith has been implicated recently in the drowning deaths of two six-year-old cousins. If you have any information regarding his whereabouts, I would greatly appreciate it if you'd call me immediately.

Samuel Lapchik

Special Agent

FAIR WARNING: We are approaching what some call a "negative thesis"— suggesting that our best theory is incapable of solving one of the most fundamental dilemmas in ethical theory, the dilemma between consequentialism and absolutism as it is illustrated so convincingly by the runaway trolley, the poor unsuspecting workers, the transplant surgeon and his players. All we can prove here is the absence of ends, that the Trolley Problem is unsolvable, insoluble, solid. Perhaps the problem is the Trolley Problem. The stories can't be cooked down to easy answers. Not even armed with superhero theories. You simply can't explain opposing moral intuitions: Bystander kills the Fat Man = OK. Surgeon kills the patient = NOT OK. Is this a problem? Perhaps intuition is, by its nature, not something that can be explained. But what else can we really trust in a pinch? Bystander lets the five die = NOT OK. Surgeon lets the five die = OK. We may have to live with this. So we answer nothing, come to no conclusions and offer no solutions. This is not a solution. This is not an answer, not a conclusion nor end. This is a celebration. A dance. A dalliance.

Have you ever been stranded with thin friends in a flooding cave-in, a Fat Man wedged in the only exit, a stick of dynamite in your hand?

Have you ever been stuck in a rowboat with strangers?

Witnessed a runaway trolley?

HERE IS THE TRUTH: We all want to be the Bystander, feel confident with our hands on the switch, and not push blindly toward ends, toward resolution. We want a reason why it feels right, but we know feelings don't obey reason. We are learning. This thing: an analytical approach. To compliment: an emotional appreciation for the stories. Left brain, right brain. So many stories. To us, it must work together— balance us somehow as we wobble between means and ends, between process and product, between sickness and health, between good and bad. We want to be the Bystander and the Surgeon somehow. We want to be released. Set free of contradiction. But we know it only gets deeper. We step. Stand. And move away from you. We've begun to realize that we are the Fat Man on the bridge and you have come for us now. You've come to take us, too. We walk away, but we wobble now, the weight too much. You've come for us and we can hear your footsteps on the bridge. We stop and grab the handrail, breathing heavily. "Stay away!" we say. "Stay back," we bark as you slip up to the rail, all friendly-like. It has come down to this. We are at the rail, waiting. You have a choice. What will you do?

We might of course have imagined it not necessary to shove the fat man... all you need to do to threaten him instead of the five is to wobble the handrail, for the handrail is low...

He is leaning on it, and wobbling it will cause him to fall over and off...

Wobbling the handrail would be impermissible, I should think— no less than shoving...

If you wobble the handrail...wobble the handrail...that is not itself an infringement...

If you wobbled the handrail...

You get the trolley to threaten him instead of them by wobbling the handrail only if, and only because, by wobbling the handrail you topple him into the path of the trolley.

Judith Jarvis Thomson
The Trolley Problem

Dear Ms. Thomson,

I used to be a highly skilled transplant surgeon. I used to be a trolley driver, a bystander, a fat man on the tracks. I used to be anything I wanted to be. I used to be a good person. I'd go to the hospital, maybe for knee surgery or some accident with a knife, and not worry about rogue doctors harvesting my organs for some Utilitarian code of ethics that commands them to maximize happiness by saving five lives, five sick lives. I used to believe that my moral intuitions were to be trusted. I had cultivated them, taught them well. But now I'm afraid to walk down the street. I see runaway trolleys in my dreams. I hear the bones of a Fat Man cracking under trolley wheels. I used to work at Dot.com Company. I used to have friends. Now I have written a four-act play I call *Bystander at the Switch* that takes place entirely within the few seconds between the time the Bystander (Me) sees the trolley and the time he pulls the switch. It's three hours long. I used to leave the house. Now I give encore performances to my cat.

I blame you for this.

I'm not sure I have the heart to be an ethical person any longer.

John Wilkes

San Francisco, CA

Where to find the heart? Because isn't that what it comes down to in the end. We can tell all the stories we want. We can talk John and Mary, X and Y; we can prepare for Smith. We can carry crib-sheets in San Francisco: Judith says, Pull the switch! We can never leave the house. But moral intuition is not so much a matter of the mind, an exercise of theory, or a search for answers in a world of Smith— but a thump of the heart, an emotional reaction to the stories of extreme situations, the moral dilemmas of this world. Bystander doesn't know, he feels what is right. That's why we like him, why we identify with his character. Transplant Surgeon thinks too much.

Smith happens.

If you are the five innocent workmen, if you are John or Mary, we want to have the heart of the Bystander and the hands of the Surgeon.

We want to believe that we could kill to save you, even if it's just one of you.

❦

MAN WALKING DOG FINDS

BODY IN ALLEY

Abandoned at birth... one child left in a phone box tried to track down the mother who discarded her in a phone box.[1]

Six a.m. Between Mulberry and Magnolia. A dropped body. Left to rot. Huddled against a truck tire. So tiny, so innocent. Sew a button to remember the spot. Stitch it to your nipple— hard and sharp with cold. The dog barks. A blast of wind stings your eyes. You tell yourself: never forget this. Never forget the purple-orange skin— brittle and dusted with the breath of a moonless morning.

"Write it down," you tell yourself. "Learn from this."

"Nothing to see here," your eyewitness says.

Wet clouds of breath hang around my head, trying to creep back inside where it's safe and musty. I whistle for the dog, absently. Preoccupied. Prenatal. Parental. I will be a father soon. This much is true here. And I want to wrap this bundle in my jacket and coo

---

[1] From "Foundlings: Abandoned at Birth" on http://www.bbc.co.uk/insideout/ northeast/series2/foundlings_abandonedbabies.shtml

softly as I rush it to the hospital. Who would do such a thing? Don't we have drop boxes now, laws to prevent abandonment? Who could just walk away?

Not me.

Not today.

I stumble through the ER doors, dragging the dog behind, screaming for nurses and doctors, clutching the body to my ribs. I want to see hot blankets unfurl in the air, great bolts of blue warmth enveloping us. Because this seems like some kind of test of my parental imagination, I conjure up IV stands whisking down linoleum halls, defibrillator paddles hopping and buzzing, syringes shooting streams of painkiller, and legions of white-coats flooding the room. They have answered my call. I want them to breathe life into this body again. I want to adopt it as my own, build a nest in our home. I want to make this body my own. But...it is only a mango dropped in a driveway, slipped out of a plastic grocery sack and left out overnight. Just a tragic frozen mango. Test or not, I would look foolish pretending it is anything more than cold fruit.

$$\mathcal{X}$$

UNPUBLISHED LETTER

TO THE

EDITOR

FROM MARY

ELDEST OF THE HOLNAM SISTERS

The data potentially demonstrates that some of the PCDDs/PCDFs in the emissions are pre-existing dioxins and furans that are vaporized out of the kiln raw feed.[1]

"Cement Kiln or Incinerator? No Holnams Barred"

"(Note: The author is a member of the Holnam's Community Advisory Committee. The views expressed here do not reflect the views of the committee or any of its other members.)"

(Note: The author is not a member of the Holnam's Community Advisory Committee. The views expressed here do not reflect views.

---

[1] All quotes are taken from the following: Trine, Cherie. "No Holnams Barred." Guest Editorial. *Bullhorn* March, 2001. This letter, which the Editors can only assume to be authentic, was nailed to a cottonwood tree just past the thirty-eighth fence post at the edge of the Holnam property. Found by a local writer, the letter was proofread, edited for grammar, punctuation, and readability, and then transcribed for public consumption.

Refract perhaps. Retire, retread. Revenge.)

"Cement kilns have become America's incinerators, one in every community."

But what do we burn? You want to know? Fingers of rebar. Bodies of concrete. The bones of streets. You ask, does Captain Smith bathe me regularly? Does he burn tires, too? Does he shell eggs with a penknife in the mornings before we children wake for work? We don't ask, for fear he might not recognize the asker. Have you ever seen him hate a stray dog?

"No plume or groundwater contamination to be traced, no legal liability. Into the air and everywhere, contaminants become part of our bodies. We pass the genetic damage to our grandkids."

You want to know how you trace plume? Is it from the feathers they drop? Captain Smith bought a peacock to keep us company. All day we shovel cement. All night we shovel rubber. The peacock struts free around the yard, chortling and cooing at us. When dusk gives way to night, we hear his talons click-clicking on the wooden porch.

This is family cement business.
You never go against the family.

"From around the country come cries for help. From Bozeman... comes a call: Holnam is trying to burn tires."

Quitting time for Captain Smith. He thumbs a matchbook. Sits on the porch, stroking his bird. Evening apple in hand. He rocks, rocks, watches us girls. Callers don't tread over now. No trace of contaminants. The Captain burns what he wants in the dark. Tosses them to the pile.

Lo, but I have seen the mound.

And it is smoldering tonight as I whisper to you through the fence that separates us.

For him, the bird dances in the dirt. Spreads her plume and shakes the colors loose.

For us, the TV burn of a tire fire is all we have.

"Ten years ago, Bozeman fought hazardous waste burning and won."

Don't you look at us and walk away. Don't pretend you didn't see it. Captain Smith preaches with promises: clean sheets, hot water, toothpaste. His heart on fire with lies. Burning rubber doesn't crackle. But it roars. What makes his waste hazardous is not speed, not quick feet, but reach— the long arms of stink. Captain's a quick trigger, a puncher, a bullet-dancer, and he sees all from the porch. Wooden rocker, back and forth. He shadowboxed for the title once. Keeps a scared pistol in his pants. Now he hardly leaves his corner.

"Communities unite to fight Holnam."

Statement of fact, a command? What do you want to hear? "Burn rubberman, burn." Captain Smith can't see our Bystander Hero, Bozeman coming, can't see the waste like the sisters can. We whisper round the kilns, tell stories of Bozeman's scarred face, broad shoulders, and white horse. Silver Guns. Leather Chaps. Rifle slung through a saddle loop.

"Right now, the really dangerous chemicals coming out of Holnam are ignored and will be ignored with tire burning."

Because we can't help gathering at the glow. Burning orange and black and thick. The Holnam Sisters sing fire songs. Roasting smores as we wait for him to sleep. His vigilant bird still struts on guard. We're ignorant as we hold our palms to the rubber heat. We are girls, our dresses stained with his soot. We roll another tire into the fire, don't notice the smell anymore.

"The most dangerous chemicals are those that persist, or break down slowly, and bioaccumulate. (Eat a fish, keep the fish's chemicals.) Some chemicals cause cellular mutations that are then passed on to future generations. Beyond cancer, many chemicals cause multi-system damage, such as nervous system damage, birth defects and learning disabilities. Hormone-mimicking chemicals, such as dioxin, cause early puberty."

Some of us have six toes. Is this what you want to hear? We menstruate at eight. (I ate a fish and kept his chemicals.) The older lungs wheeze beyond cancer. Hair is a painted luxury for some— more often wigs made from discarded mops.

Tire hammocks hang from every branch. Here we sleep, curled up in rubber bunks. Tonight the trees will squirm from the weight of our dreams. Our cradles will rock.

Clickety-clickety-click. The peacock struts below. Keeping guard.

We dream stories of a wooden horse. Bozeman and a pack of ponies. Galloping.

One for each of us. Running from the burn, the Captain, the bird.

ᗝ

APOLOGY TO
HENRY AARON

Fig. 1: [REDACTED] Hank Aaron trots around bases after record setting home run #715 in 1974. A white fan who jumped from the stands appears in the left corner of the picture, running hard, head down, and wearing what appears to be a backpack.

Henry Aaron, when you smacked home run number 715 into the lights, fans dropped to the evergreen field and ran after you. I know you've seen the film footage that I've seen, pictures that promised a moment of pure joy. The roar of the crowd. The drop of jaws. The drop of drinks and hot dogs. This one white fan— his wild hair flying and toothy smile. The first one there. He jumps from his seat. Legs pumping, he gallops for the infield. You trot around the bases, waving to the crowd. You've just knocked the Babe from his throne. You don't even see him coming. And he's just this loose-limbed image of happiness— or at least that's what I thought, that's what I believed.

He must have seen the home run before it even left your bat, right in mid-swing. The swipe of the stick, the path of the ball— and he knew Ruth's record was gone. I imagine he'd been following your record march, chalking up dingers on his wall at home, maybe scratching them into the back of his bedroom door. He could be nineteen years old, still living in his widowed mother's basement. For a ticket to the game, maybe he traded his most prized possession— a miniature bicycle built for him by his Chinese neighbor. Maybe he loved this bicycle with its tiny rubber-band tires, spokes made from copper wire, and a frame bent from a clothes hanger. Maybe this man and his neighbor watched you Saturdays on television. He taught her words like *strike, ball, bullpen, fastball, slider*. She taught him the secret of silence, the trick to dancing with houseflies. His mother paid her for piano lessons. But the teacher sat beside him on the bench while he practiced. Her hand on his leg, her finger reading the inseam of his jeans, she whispered the play-by-play from your baseball games. She whispered words she had memorized from game-day recordings he slipped into her mailbox after dark. *Aaron steps up to the plate. The two-two pitch. He swings. And, oh baby, it's outta here.* She made miniature toys she could have sold to emperors. She built a tiny bicycle for two. She told stories with her hands.

But now... she would never forgive this foolish man who skipped his lesson, left her arms, pushed his way up to the wall, and waited for the hard crack of ball to bat. What about the bicycle between them? There's nothing musical about his leaving. But for him it was always about you, Henry Aaron. He would have given anything for this moment, even a bicycle token. Maybe like me as a child, this white boy dreamed only of black heroes. Maybe he, too, read only biographies of black athletes. His mother probably didn't understand why it was so important. She never knew a thing of Babe Ruth, the white giant. She sat at home, reluctantly tuning her radio to the game. And maybe all of this would make a difference if it were true.

Whatever the reason, whatever he left behind, this man was there to see your swing, Henry. He had a jump on the ball and ran hard to catch you between second and third base. You just trotted around the diamond, waving to the crowd, not gloating about it. That wasn't your way. And then he burst into the picture and slapped you hard on the shoulder. You turned at the last second. And I like to imagine that he called you "Mr. Aaron." I wish he'd said something beautiful— something to fit the image given me by the television cameras. I don't know what he was thinking. But I do know now what you thought. I've heard your words recently, Mr. Aaron.

What should have been your proudest moment had already been soiled by repeated phone calls to your home, threats whispered into the receiver. And I believed that this young man, stupid with joy, his limbs all loose in the rush of pride, just wanted to share your triumph— as if he was saying for all of us, you are the greatest. But you, Henry Aaron— just for a split second— you believed that he had come to kill you, put a bullet in your head right there on the field in front of teammates and the world. I heard your words some twenty years later, saw this moment through different eyes. I realized again the false promises of television. And I apologize for this fan— for his grin, his gait, his slap. I apologize for his dreams, his color, and my belief. I apologize to his imaginary Chinese lover. I apologize because it sounds like lies. I apologize for writing. But there's something about your memory I just can't shake.

WILL THE REAL

K. NELSON

PLEASE STAND UP?

K. Nelson took only two English courses as an undergraduate... Although he went on to earn a degree in environmental law... Nelson has never practiced law. Instead, he has supported himself over the years with a series of part-time jobs as a tennis professional, city judge, travel agent, squash coach, bartender, and farmhand. More recently, Nelson has worked intermittently as a distinguished visiting professor at various universities... An avid bird-watcher, he has recorded more than 670 species on his "life list." Much of Nelson's fiction is concerned with birds...[1]

K. Nelson is not a figment of my imagination. I've seen him before; but at one point I began to question whether he really exists. He's a writer and he came to town once and gave a public reading from his work. I think. It was a story about a seriously conflicted man running uphill— literally running. I recall the rhythm of his prose and the way it mimicked the rhythm of the footsteps. There was a view from a mountain trail down into a valley

---

[1] Quotes from K. Nelson's Contributor Note in *An Anthology of Nature Writing*

and a tiny wooden cabin belching smoke from a stone chimney. There was a woman in the window wringing her hands, a woman left behind.

K. had a good reading voice, a nice stage presence. The rhythm of the prose was like a pulse beating inside our narrator. The man was in love with the woman. I don't remember much else. But I had fleeting images of K. Nelson, the writer. He was handsome in the wiry rugged western way— longish hair, tan, thin, tall, and bright-eyed. He loved birds. He'd written several books. He'd written about birds and tennis. He was a "name"; and I suppose that's why I contacted him in the first place. He was a regional writer with prestigious awards (an Edward Abbey Prize, a NEA, and some Pushcart nominations), a name to fill seats and make everyone happy.

That was my job one night a month. I made people happy. Sometimes. I ran the Poetry and Prose Series at a tiny old community theatre in downtown Fort Collins, Colorado. The house seated 50, maybe 60 with some overflow; and I tried to fill it for every reading. It could be a difficult job. Sometimes the audience didn't show despite my admittedly meager publicity efforts, and writers were asked to give a reading to seventeen (or seven) people.

Fear of audience no-show's was one thing. Sometimes when the theatre was full and the clock winding down close to 7:30, I had this gut fear that the writer wouldn't show. But they always came strolling in a few minutes late. They'd always showed. So far.

We started planning the fall series in July and I sent an email to K. Nelson at K.nelson@yahoo.com. I had remembered him from the reading he gave, recalled that he had a number of books and lived in Colorado; so I decided to make contact. I don't remember where I found the address; but I've been wracking my brain to recall. Some website somewhere. Or was it a friend who gave it to me? I still don't know for sure. Somebody recommended him; and my message went out to him, bottled up in binary code, floating free on waves– disseminating in the wash of information. That's when it all began.

CORRESPONDENCE

From: Steven Church <swcras@juno.com>
To: K. Nelson <K.nelson@yahoo.com>
Subject: Bas Bleu Reading

Dear K.,

My name is Steven Church and I am a co-coordinator for the Poetry and Prose Series at the Bas Bleu Theatre in Fort Collins. I was fortunate enough to attend your reading a few years ago at CSU, when I was a first-semester MFA student; and I was hoping you might be interested in reading at the Bas Bleu this Fall. We can't offer much in terms of compensation, just a measly $50, but it's a great venue and we usually bring in some good crowds. We also work with our local independent bookstore to make sure we have books for sale at the reading. Please let me know if you'd be interested.

Thanks. -- Steven Church

Simultaneously a message sizzled loose from my synapses and I caught bits of the news from my neurotransmitters, missives from my subconscious. Regular reports kept coming and they rang with self-doubt.

From: "S.S." <swakeup@yuno.com>
To: Steven Church <swcras@juno.com>
Subject: Re: Bas Bleu Reading

Dear Steve,

You think you're so cool, think you have everything organized, without seeming too organized, just artistic enough to fool everyone. Do you really think he cares that you were "a first-semester MFA student"? You're just trying to kiss ass. You can call it "networking" if you want, but we all know what this really is. If you pay attention from this point forward, I will be trying to suggest that perhaps you've missed something, some key component of effective and responsible communication; but you're already resistant to my efforts. You're such a lazy communicator. How can you be sure he received your message? Email is so impersonal, don't you think? You could have at least called. What? Are you afraid of the phone or something, afraid of Mr. K. Nelson, award-winning writer, teacher, traveler, and lover? Perhaps you feel inadequate, like a loser compared to K. Nelson in his running shorts, K. Nelson in his woolly Irish sweater, K. Nelson killing a bear, K. Nelson adding species to his "life list," K. Nelson writing novel after novel or effortlessly pumping out memoirs of his youth. That's just ridiculous. You're ridiculous.

Just checking in.
Best Wishes. -- Subconscious

Confession of a Word Lover

It was true. I found the telephone troublesome and often preferred to contact writers through e-mail. But e-mail is a strange animal, a uniquely challenging form of human interaction, a refuge for liars and frauds, a vehicle for spreading viruses and other sickness, and also completely indispensable to people like me.

Some days when my mailbox was loading up and I spent more time typing than talking, I wondered how we ever got along without it. Was our need for constant communication a product of the technology, or vice versa? I wondered what other form of communication allows you to say so much and take so little responsibility for it. It was a little dangerous and too easy for someone like me, someone who obsessed about words, easier than small talk sometimes— probably because words come more naturally for me in print. It was in email that I talked off the top of my head, more than in any other medium. I rambled and babbled in writing, and really had to watch my mouth sometimes.

There was nobody to see or hear my words, no check of facial features nor nonverbal cues to inappropriate behavior, no awareness of the reader's state of mind, their receptiveness to your message. Didn't we call them email messages instead of letters because they're more like something we scribble down on a scrap of paper, stuff into a bottle, and drop in the ocean than something we thoughtfully create, seal in an envelope, and drop in a mailbox?

I often second-guessed myself with email more than any other form of communication. I'd pull up messages from my SENT box to double or even triple check what I'd said. That was the paradoxical part, too. It was so easy to send, so impossible to take back, but always there for you to see. This didn't happen with the telephone or a letter. As a culture, we were still learning how to use what was perhaps our most common and consistent form of human interaction. I know I was still learning what could and could not be accomplished through email. I was learning how well you could know someone electronically and what you could never know. As my father always said, it's not what you know, it's who you know that makes all the difference.

But what if we never really know anybody again?

CORRESPONDENCE

From: "S.S." <swakeup@yuno.com>
To: Steven Church <swcras@juno.com>
Subject: Soapbox

Dear Stevie,

Jesus, get off you're fucking soapbox. Call off the dogs. We get it, all right! You have some issue with human interaction. You can't handle normal everyday anonymous electronic communication. You used to be afraid of the phone. I'm surprised you didn't tell them how you still sweat like a sailor every time you speak in public— even though you do it all the time. Maybe you should have mentioned something about your grandfather's weekly letter to the family; the one he pounded out on a Smith-Corona typewriter every week down in the basement and signed "Pop." That would have been a perfect opportunity to make some interesting connections, perhaps some metaphorical unity and depth in an otherwise shallow diatribe. Perhaps you could have mentioned your fascination with your grandfather's typewriters and the way the letter-arms flung up and smacked the carriage so violently. You could have talked about the tactile element of communication. But you blew it babbling about "culture." Do you think K. Nelson wastes his time writing about communication and culture? K. Nelson can kill large mammals with his bare hands. K. Nelson kayaks whitewater rivers. K. Nelson understands all these things about email that seem too revolutionary to you; he understands them, digests them, and craps them out. You just can't leave it well enough alone. K. Nelson doesn't own a computer. K. Nelson hires personal assistants to check his email. He's too busy watching birds.

Talk with you soon.

Subconscious

Maybe

After I sent that first message to K. Nelson, I didn't hear anything for days and had started to worry (just a little). At first I thought I might have made an honest mistake. Perhaps I had addressed the message wrong. Perhaps I hadn't been clear in my wording. Maybe his mailbox was full. Maybe he was the kind of writer who didn't appreciate email correspondence— like friends I know who can barely turn their computer on and off, professors who still compose massive 400-page tomes on a typewriter.

I dropped names like I knew I should, playing all my public relations cards— in other words "kissing ass." But it was all right there— the reference to a reading here in the past, a specific mention of his friend, and some half-assed praise of his work. When his response did finally come, however late and notable for its brevity, it implied with silence that he was, at least, the very same K. Nelson I had seen in a banquet room in the Student Center. That much I could be sure of. Right?

CORRESPONDENCE

From: K. Nelson <K.nelson@yahoo.com>

To: Steven Church <swcras@juno.com>

Subject: Re: Bas Bleu Reading

Dear Steven,

Thank you for your kind invitation. I would be very pleased to read at the Bas Bleu Festival!

Let's make certain that the dates do not conflict. Please contact me by telephone to follow up on the arrangements.

Warmest regards,

K. Nelson

CORRESPONDENCE

From: "S.S." <swakeup@yuno.com>
To: Steven Church <swcras@juno.com>
Subject: Re: Re: Bas Bleu Reading

Dear Stevie,

Are you blind? Obviously he doesn't appreciate email conversation. Jesus, look at what he says, "contact me by telephone." I don't care if he didn't give you his number. That's not his problem. That's your problem. That's the problem with email, isn't it? So informal. Such lack of responsibility. Can't you just see K. Nelson sitting by his stone fireplace, clucking his tongue at you? He makes fun of you to his hounds, laughing and spilling his snifter of brandy. K. Nelson tells all his buddies at the tennis club about your insolence, the young whippersnapper who thinks he can just fire off an email out of the blue to K. Nelson, award winning writer. K. Nelson doesn't appreciate your name-dropping and ass-kissing. He sees right through your transparent efforts to impress him. K. Nelson doesn't want to read another email from you. K. Nelson makes mochas in his kitchen after his morning run. K. Nelson is old enough to be your father, but he's in better shape than you'll ever be. K. Nelson is a professional. K. Nelson has the decency to communicate like a mature adult.

Warmest regards,
Subconscious

Festival of What

In my mild panic for contact and control, I began to wonder what to make of his mention of festival? Was this an early attempt to shake my confidence, cause me to question myself? At the time it did stand out to me. Writers aren't involved with too many festivals. It makes it sound like some kind of all-day affair with bands and kegs and kids with glow-sticks, T-shirt and burrito salesmen, dudes riding coolers on a skateboard selling beer for a buck. And I'm sure I never used that word festival in reference to the reading. What is he expecting? At this point I was already thinking he's a little strange for asking me to call but not giving me a phone number. But a lot of writers are strange. I was more worried about his expectations for atmosphere. I briefly contemplated writing (or calling) him to clarify that there will be, in fact, no festival when he reads at the Bas Bleu Theatre.

CORRESPONDENCE

From: Steven Church <swcras@juno.com>
To: K. Nelson <K.nelson@yahoo.com>
Subject: Re: Re: Re: Bas Bleu Reading

Dear K.,

That's great! I'm glad you'd like to join us. Unfortunately I don't have your phone number to follow up. I'll try to find it. But failing that, how would Nov. 13 work for you? It's a Wednesday. I think we will pair you with another fiction writer, Karen Palmer. It should be a great reading! If not then, we have some dates open in the Spring, too. Just give me your number, and I'll call to make arrangements.

Thanks.

Best. – Steve

On Hold

Several days later and I was still waiting for a phone number, still telling myself not to worry. I tried in vain to find one attached to his name; but I didn't panic, not yet. Perhaps K. Nelson is just one of those eccentric writers. Maybe he can't seem to deal with life in the twentieth century and pines for the days of manual typewriters and the telegraph wire. He may lament the loss of the Pony Express, the decline of railroad transportation, the reluctance of people to pen letters nowadays.

I read somewhere that K. Nelson has written a novel about tennis. I didn't know if it was about the poetry and beauty of the sport, or if a tennis player just plays prominently in the novel. But I imagined long and detailed descriptions of the game, rife with physiology and the mechanics of movement. There would be lots of green. There would be talk of geometry, the angles of success, and historic matches between Jimmy Connors and John McEnroe. There might be a tennis pro named Mitch who humps socialite women for sport.

For some reason I pictured K. Nelson the writer as Mitch, not some character. He had wispy sandy-brown hair, white shorts, and a white sweatband across his forehead. He was smacking balls on a pristine green court situated on a palatial mountain estate. I speculated that maybe he wears the sweatband when he writes, perspiring over every magnificent word.

I didn't know that. I didn't know anything about him really—nothing at all. I remembered him being tall, sort of athletic, and good-looking— the kind of face meant for a book jacket. He carried himself with great confidence. He could have been an actor. He could have been an international man of mystery. I imagined him storming into town in a WWII biplane, a white scarf trailing behind. He removed his goggles and leather jacket then recited a story from memory while men shuddered and swooning women tossed their panties on stage.

CORRESPONDENCE

To: Steven Church <swcras@juno.com>
From: K. Nelson <K.nelson@yahoo.com>
Subject: Re: Re: Re: Bas Bleu Reading

Looks good on my calendar, Steve. Is there a theme I might wish to adhere to in the reading? Just let me know the details and I'll work it out at this end.

Regards,
K.

From: "S.S." <swakeup@yuno.com >
To: Steven Church <swcras@juno.com>
Subject: Re: Re: Re: Re: Bas Bleu Reading

Stevie,

Can't you see where this is leading yet? You're so busy worrying about yourself, taking liberties with K. Nelson, that you're probably missing the subtext in all of this. Don't you feel so superior, talking about those poor anachronistic writers who can't keep up with the pace of the world? There is a theme developing here— something about hubris and tennis, words and miscommunication. Games are being played. K. Nelson stands on a green court at dusk. He's wearing his white tennis shorts and lobbing fuzzy yellow balls at your head; but you seem to have your pants around your ankles, your hands full of yourself, because they're bouncing off your skull and landing at your feet. You're missing it entirely.

Bristly Regards,
Subconscious

THEMATIC UNITY

I was beginning to feel good here, confident and efficient. One down, two more readings to fill for the Fall Series. I was on top of things, working on cruise control to handle publicity and I just ignored the nagging buzz of my subconscious. I was the Man, the Shiznit, the Email Master— inundating lists with clever announcements for the reading, reminding people to, "tell their friends, neighbors, pets, and invisible playmates." K. would read with another novelist from Colorado. We'd have books for sale. We'd have cream soda, water-crackers, and cheese cubes. We'd have a theatre full of people eating water-crackers and cheese cubes. People love cheese cubes.

I didn't really think twice of his question about themes. I've never been to a theme reading; but maybe this is something common to big name writers with books and good looks. Maybe the other author had a story about tennis or something athletic. They could both read wearing headbands and holding tennis rackets. It could be like this Billie Jean King versus Bobby Riggs kind of thing… or not.

CORRESPONDENCE

To: Steven Church <swcras@juno.com>
From: K. Nelson <K.nelson@yahoo.com>
Subject: Re: Re: Re: Bas Bleu Reading

K.,

Great to hear! No special theme but you will be reading with another Colorado novelist and CCA winner. Steven Schwartz has said very nice things about both of you and the much-anticipated reading. The reading will begin at 7:30 and is typically followed by a brief Q&A session with the audience and a small reception. We work with our local bookstore here in town to make sure we have books for sale. I'll be sure to contact Ellen about ordering yours. If you could send me some press materials, maybe a picture and some reviews, even a review copy or two, I can make sure we have posters and so forth. My home address is 7281 W. Magnolia St. Fort Collins, 80524. Bas Bleu is located at 216 Pine St. in Old Town Fort Collins. Their phone number is 798-8949. If you give me a mailing address I'll send you copies of our posters and a map if you need it. Looking forward to reading and hearing your work again!

Thanks.
—Steven

From: "S.S." <swakeup@yuno.com >
To: Steven Church <swcras@juno.com>
Subject: Re: Re: Re: Re: Bas Bleu Reading

Hey Stevie,

Look at you, throwing out names, numbers, and addresses like you know this guy. You're so considerate. Maybe you're hoping K. Nelson will stop by the house in his tennis shorts and offer to take you out hunting for large mammals or maybe for an afternoon of birdwatching. He won't. K. Nelson is too busy for that kind of nonsense. He has books to write, fans to please. He doesn't have much time for the likes of you; and he won't call or send anything in the mail. That's just the way K. Nelson behaves.

Chow,
Subconscious

p.s. That itchy restless feeling you've been getting lately, the one that keeps you up at night pacing in front of the window; that's my work. Nice, huh?

To: Steven Church <swcras@juno.com>
From: K. Nelson <K.nelson@yahoo.com>
Subject: Re: Re: Re: Bas Bleu Reading

Thanks Steve,
I'll see what I can scare up for materials and get them over to you...
then I'll block out that date on my calendar.

I look forward to a fun and lively reading.

Take care,
K.

BLOCKING IT OUT

A fun and lively reading sounded great. He's blocking out the date and this seemed like a good way to close our communication for the time. Three months passed... and suddenly it was October, just a few weeks away from the reading. I sent out another email to K. and the other novelist, reminding them of the reading, expressing my genuine excitement about the event. I was on top of things—organized, efficient, and altogether impressive. The other novelist responded almost immediately. She was excited to participate. She was looking forward to it.

I got nothing from K. Nelson, nothing at all; but I didn't think much of it at first. Eccentric tennis playing writers who wear headbands when they compose would probably act like that. I'd expect him to keep me guessing a little, wondering if he'll really show.

Eventually, as the date neared, I began to do just that. I started to doubt myself all over again, believing that I had failed to confirm dates and times with K.; but I didn't yet go back through my old emails. I wouldn't go so far as to confirm my mistakes; finding it easier instead to believe that K. Nelson would come flying into town unannounced and swoop into the theatre just five minutes before show time.

I believed this right up until I got a disturbing note from a woman married to a professor in the English department, a woman I took a class with once, who is involved in some kind of poetry therapy practice. I remember her talking a lot about tennis and how much she loved Wimbledon. She and her husband watched a lot of tennis. They were big fans of the game. They spent their summers watching tennis. They were old friends of K. Nelson. Perhaps they played together, lobbing volleys back and forth, sipping wine coolers between points, and lamenting the demise of the sports novel. I don't really know. All I know is that she lobbed an email at me that hit me square in the nose, knocking me loopy for a moment; and I had to gather myself before I could even consider a return volley.

CORRESPONDENCE

From: Joannah Merriman <jetlost@lamar.acns.colostate.edu>
To: Steven Church <swcras@juno.com>
Subject: Re: Cost of Admission to Bas Bleu

Dear Steven: I have a very large question about this reading next Wednesday. Your e-mail states that one of the authors is K. Nelson, author of <u>Language in the Blood</u>, etc. K. is a very good friend of ours, and is teaching in Texas this semester. He just spoke to Neil last week and didn't mention the reading, so I e-mailed him inviting him to stay at our house since he would be here next week to read for Bas Bleu. He just responded saying he has no idea what we are talking about. What's up?

Joannah Merriman

P.S. I'll forward you his response to me.

A very large question indeed. If questions were primates it would be an eight hundred pound gorilla sitting on my chest, smacking me in the face with his rough and meaty paw. I got this email at work and it sent me into a minor panic attack. I nearly passed out on my desk.

The questions raced: Did I forget to confirm dates and times?

Did he forget? What went wrong? Blasted email. Something got lost, tangled up in the mass of wires and satellites, swept under in tides of information. My stomach churned. He probably got ten emails a day from pathetic series coordinators begging for his presence, editors bidding for his latest work, or tennis fans wanting to buy out-of-print copies of his brilliant novel.

From: "S.S." <swakeup@yuno.com >
To: Steven Church <swcras@juno.com>
Subject: Re: Re: Re: Re: Bas Bleu Reading

Hey Stevie,

You're close, Stevie boy. But not quite there yet. You still think it's all about you— that fail or succeed it's all within your control. But once you plug those messages into bottles and toss them into the tides, it's out of your hands. You give up those words and only have minimal control over how they will be received. Look back at your transmissions, read the words. You'll see. You did everything you could, didn't you? I mean, what did he expect? Were you supposed to come knocking on his door with a personalized invitation sealed in wax and addressed in calligraphy?

Rusty Regards,
Subconscious

MISUNDERESTIMATE

I quickly decided that there was nothing left to do but just move on. K. Nelson would not be flying into town, parachuting into the street in front of the theatre. K. Nelson was in Texas teaching cowboys how to be tough, or teaching writers how to invent tough cowboys. He was bagging birds for his "Life List." K. Nelson cared nothing for my predicament. He probably found the whole thing quite amusing. He probably thought I was some solicitor, some purveyor of junk mail and penis-enhancing products. But of course K. Nelson wouldn't need any of that. He wouldn't need any enhancement. There he sat in Texas, chuckling over my dumb luck, feeling little pity; and I couldn't really blame him for this. He was K. Nelson, semi-famous writer and tennis player. He had bigger things to worry about than our little reading series.

From: Steven Church <swcras@juno.com>
To: Joannah Merriman <jetlost@lamar.acns.colostate.edu>
Subject: Re: Cost of Admission to Bas Bleu

Joannah,
Ouch, that's really horrible news. Below is the email I received from him months ago. He didn't mention anything about being in Texas. I've been using this email (K.nelson@yahoo.com) and have had trouble getting in touch with him. He asked that I call him, but

never gave me a phone number. I sent another email to confirm but never received a response. Perhaps you have an email that he checks regularly? I guess we'll just have to wing it without him.

—Steven

I began the process of trying to find a last minute replacement for K. Nelson, convinced that I had failed horribly in my duties as Reading Series Coordinator. At first I didn't go back through my old emails, probably not wanting to remind myself of my mistakes. Somewhere along the way communication failed, the lines severed, and I just left it like that...for a day or two.

But then something starting nagging me, pulling at my sense of curiosity. Or perhaps it was just my desire to vindicate myself and blame someone else. I finally returned to my old transmissions, reading carefully and finding that I'd actually done all that I could to maintain contact with Mr. K. Nelson. There wasn't much else I could do. So I began to blame K. Nelson and his smarmy attitude, his cavalier forgetting of obligations, his preoccupation with tennis and birds. It was HIS fault. I convinced myself that he was one of those pompous writer-types who felt entitled to star treatment, the sort of guy who blows off readings or commitments and forgives these actions as those of an "eccentric."

This is when I got a short note from the writer, K. Nelson— the one I'd seen read his story about the running man and the lonely woman— explaining that his email address is, in fact, K.snelson@

yahoo.com, and that he hadn't received anything from me regarding the reading series.

The first time he heard about the reading was when his friend Joanna mentioned it in her email and offered him a place to stay for the night. The other K. Nelson, the individual attached to the email address K.nelson@yahoo.com, was of no relation to him.

He was a fraud, a fake, a fakir, a phony, an imposter.

"He is not me," Mr. Nelson said.

The real K. Nelson told me that he'd missed out on an opportunity to attend a conference last year because an agent had tried to contact him using the K.nelson@yahoo.com address and was never clued into the fact that he had contacted the wrong K. Nelson.

Apparently this other K. Nelson liked to pretend he was K. Nelson— writer, tennis player, marathoner, birder and writer of novels. He liked to believe that he was something more, the kind of man who gets requests from strangers for his presence in faraway cities. I imagine that he'd enjoyed toying with me, stringing me along and telling all his buddies about the rube he buffaloed in Colorado, the idiot who believed anything he read in e-mail format.

CORRESPONDENCE

From: "S.S." <swakeup@yuno.com >
To: Steven Church <swcras@juno.com>
Subject: Re: Re: Re: Re: Bas Bleu Reading

Hey Stevie,

Well, well you've finally made it, right? You think you've got him all figured out. There he is, sad and lonely, the other K. Nelson spending hours on the web watching porn. He gets these strange notes from some punk in Colorado, some guy willing to shell out his address and other information to any old K. Nelson, and he figures he can have some fun with this. Sure, he could just send a quick email explaining that he's not the real K. Nelson. He's the other K. Nelson and he has several cloudy fish tanks in his apartment, where all of the inhabitants are named after comic book characters. You see him toying with you, don't you Stevie? All your self-confidence was so fragile, so transitory; and he watched it come crashing down-- that wicked pendulum swing in your life from confidence to doubt, arrogance to ignorance. Swinging back and forth. He messed with your head.

What are you going to do about it?

Pointed Regards,
Subconscious

SWEET REVENGE

I guess I wanted to let the fake K. Nelson know that I was on to him. I wanted to get in a shot or two without admitting that he'd made a fool of me. I wanted some kind of revenge— as petty as that sounds— or at least a chance to keep playing the game. I'm a competitive guy and I don't play nice when I get poked in the eye. I poke back.

I really didn't want the fake K. Nelson to think he rattled me; and that's when I began to realize the beauty of email communication— the anonymity, the freedom, and the control. He couldn't see my facial expressions, couldn't witness my embarrassment, but could only imagine what I must have been feeling. He needed me. He could only use what I fed him.

So I began the crafting of words, the sculpting of a response. Everything so deliberate, so intentional. I could say exactly what I wanted to say, nothing more, and there was no mitigation by facial expressions or body language. Imagine a conversation that lasts for days. You took a few sentences, wrote them down, and disappeared for hours before returning with a response. It was more like a debate, a rhetorical exercise, than a true conversation. Sarcasm was easy to miss because it wasn't highlighted by the tone of voice, the exaggerated inflexions. You had to speculate more. What does he mean by that?

I realized slowly that the instrument of my downfall, email, could also be the instrument of my salvation. Perhaps I could scavenge some dignity from the wreck around me and find a way to milk this experience for something larger. What I didn't realize is that the fake K. Nelson wanted to play, too.

CORRESPONDENCE

From: Steven Church <swcras@juno.com>
To: K. Nelson <K.nelson@yahoo.com>
Subject: Re: Re: Re: Re: Bas Bleu Reading

Dear K.,
I apologize for this, but I'm afraid your reading at the Bas Bleu Festival on Nov. 13 has been canceled. The theatre has been overrun by feral cats. Sorry for the inconvenience.

Steve

From: K. Nelson <K.nelson@yahoo.com>
To: Steven Church <swcras@juno.com>
Subject: La fiesta de Reses Muertas del Gato

Hey Steve,
Don't worry!   That's OK... It was going to be a long flight for me coming from Miami anyway.

Too bad about the feline carcasses littering 'da joint.   What happened?   Did Tom Clancy read one of his tepid works and the rank fumes of his piquant manuscript killed the poor little critters as they listened?

I must admit that I am disappointed about not being able to read from my work. I was going to start with my newest work entitled "Ode to a Commode". It's a seminal piece that I think will finally shatter the myth that you can't any longer sell a novel that's written strictly in Iambic Pentameter.

You'll miss having me. ;-)

Try me next year, after I come back from my annual pilgrimage to the Nude Film Festival held in Sans Vêtements, France.

C'est la vie.

K. S. Nelson
Miami, Florida

PLAYING ALONG

My subconscious sizzled and popped. Fires flared in my skull. Neurons burst like pine trees boiling with sap, and I was burning for this guy. I didn't think he even knew what "feral" meant, but he used words like "piquant." My competitive engine began to churn and I could hardly believe his unabashed bravado. "Ode to a Commode"? Really? If we were on the basketball court, I would've said something about his mother and given him an elbow to the ribs. But this wasn't a physical contest. This was a mental game. He understood email, the power of his anonymity, and it was nothing new to him, not some revolutionary realization. He'd been playing this game all along and I was just catching up... bzzzz, pop, pop. He was still two steps ahead of me. He knew that I knew that he was not the real K. Nelson; but he couldn't let me know that he knew that I knew.

At some point I felt a shift in my understanding of these events, a slide from confusion into curiosity. I began to hope that this game would go on forever, that we'd maintain this fictional relationship, and he would send me updates on his seminal work, "Ode to a Commode," and we'd discuss the challenge of marketing a novel about toilets written in iambic pentameter. Maybe he would've admitted that he doesn't really like tennis that much and that he never killed a bear. I could've asked him about the sweatbands and his "life list." We could've talked about fiction and how it lets you live other lives; and both of us would've understood the irony of it, but we'd never admit it. I would've scheduled fake readings with other famous authors in strange places— public restrooms, country churches, and bus stations— and maybe the fake K. Nelson would've sent me fabricated promotional materials and fictionalized book reviews. We could've gone on like this forever.

CORRESPONDENCE

To: K. Nelson <K.snelson@yahoo.com> a.k.a. The Real K. Nelson
From: Steven Church <swcras@juno.com>
Subject: Bas Bleu Reading

Dear K.,

Don't know if you care, but I sent an email to the other K. Nelson to "cancel" his reading engagement and this was his response (see above). Apparently he thinks it's quite funny to pretend to be someone he's not. You might want to change your email address.

Steve

To: Steven Church <swcras@juno.com>
From: K. Nelson <K.snelson@yahoo.com>
Subject: Re: Bas Bleu Reading

Steven,

I think Joannah forwarded the message to me... I agree it was pretty nervy. I've been in touch with the other guy, and to be fair, he didn't have any address to forward mail to me. Still...

Hope we can work out a reading after the new book comes out.

K.

DROP IT

This just kept getting more unbelievable. I could hardly countenance this response from the real K. Nelson. What was he thinking? It didn't seem to bother him at all that the fake K. Nelson was pretending to be him, assuming his identity or at least not rejecting it. He didn't seem to care that he was being made to look like an ass who uses words like "piquant" and jokes about a toilet novel written in iambic pentameter. He'd even been in contact with the other K. Nelson. What did that mean? This had happened before. What did he say?

I imagined them having a good chuckle over the whole thing and planning a tennis date in Miami. All the other guy had to do was send a quick note to me saying I'd got the wrong K. Nelson. It wasn't a difficult thing to do. The fake K. Nelson liked the attention, I thought; and who wouldn't? You get an email from a stranger praising your artistic talent and your awe-inspiring presence. Anyone would be tempted— even for just a second— to slip into that identity; and it was so easy with email, just a few choice words and the click of a button. But it would still bother me if someone had assumed my electronic identity. I would've at least considered changing my email address.

Perhaps the real K. Nelson is so confident in his identity, so oblivious, that he finds it somehow flattering? I didn't know and I suppose I never will. The twists of this story just kept getting more and more unpredictable. At some point I decided it was better just to go along for the ride. After his response to my "cancellation" of the reading, I couldn't just leave it alone. I had to respond.

Correspondence

To: K. Nelson <K.nelson@yahoo.com>
From: Steven Church <swcras@juno.com>
Subject: Re: La fiesta de Reses Muertas de Gato

Hey K.,

Boy, that is a shame. Our audience is hungry for seminal works about commodes. And I've actually heard that iambic pentameter is the hot form these days. In fact, Teri Gross was interviewing Salmon Rushdie on Fresh Air the other day about his latest venture, a pornographic retelling of Kafka's Metamorphosis written in iambic pentameter.

By the way, how's your new memoir coming? I heard through the grapevine that it has something to do with travels in Mongolia, amputees, and fecal obsession. Sounds absolutely riveting!

And since you're so disappointed about not reading, perhaps we can go ahead and reschedule? I'll pencil you in for Bastille Day, 2006. Come dressed as a French pastry and read something about cats. I'll call to confirm :)

Your friend and fan. -- Steve

CRUMBLE

My missive washed around in the electronic sea, lost amidst the digital plankton, and never landed on shore— at least not in the way I had hoped. I was so proud of myself, so sure I'd get a rise out of him, so confident I'd get the last laugh. But I waited for days and got no response from the fake K. Nelson. Nothing. No witty retort. No further fictions. He just quit playing the game— and it hardly seemed fair. He wouldn't feed me a thing. I wanted to wallow in lies a little longer. I wanted to keep up the facades because, in the end, perhaps it was more real than anything else.

To: Steven Church <swcras@juno.com>
From:"SS" Subconscious <swakeup@yuno.com>
Subject: The End

Stevie,

I guess you figured you'd meet crazy with crazy. Nice volley. Though I can't help but notice a lingering bitterness; perhaps the after-taste of an ego-check? I guess you figured the fake K. Nelson plays tennis too, or at least understands the game. He lives in Miami after all; and he's still lobbing fuzzy yellow balls at your head. But at least you've got your pants up now, your racquet in hand, and there's nothing left to do but keep swinging those big words around.

Hopeful regards,
Subconscious

A VICTIM OF SHOES

Although simply called boots or sandals by young women, the media dubbed these "Oiran Shoes," after the high-ranking courtesans of the feudal period, called Oiran, who wore tall lacquered footwear for special promenades. Mega-platforms have been blamed for accidents, injuries, and even the death of a woman in 1999. In that instance, the victim fell and fractured her skull because she had just purchased the shoes and was not accustomed to wearing them.[1]

Sighting one of these girls is like catching a glimpse of a rare and strange creature...

–Laura Miller

Walking on city streets, the Yamamba Girl falls from her shoes. You stop to listen— the dial tuned to NPR, plugged into Tokyo city. You cannot not listen. Even in the double negative space between sound and sense.

---

[1] From *Beauty Up: Exploring Contemporary Japanese Body Aesthetics*, by Laura Miller

To survive, citizens banished the unproductive elderly to the mountains to die. Japanese legend holds that these mountain women would come down to raid the towns for food.

This is what you know: the girl wears silver hair stiff as wire, white lipstick, white eye shadow. Glitter cheeked, tattooed, she teeters in ten-inch platform boots— knee-high, shiny chrome zipper, blue leather mini-skirt and a fuzzy white lamb's sweater. Hello Kitty lunch box, backpack, and knee socks. She is fierce and fragile— like a translucent fawn, newly freed from her glass menagerie.

Bad little boys and girls who don't mind their parents are often told that they will be taken away in the night by the ghostly yamamba.[2]

Named for a mythical mountain witch, the Yamamba Girl towers on stilts over girls in normal shoes. She is so much larger now. Bigger than the tiny flat where her family lives. Too big for her shared bedroom, her desk at school, or that grey wool dress her mother wants her to wear. Too big for the clucking tongues, the rules, the cages. Too big.

But she is unpracticed, unsteady in her Oiran. She is falling, tipping, swaying. You reach. But you

[2] From "Japanese 'Mountain Hag Fashion' the New Trend" at www.weirdasianews. com

cannot stop the tip and tilt. It's an epidemic now. A heel trapped in sidewalk crack, she falls before your eyes over and over again.

You only hear words filtered through a radio translator.

But you imagine ruined knees, shattered dreams of American pop life. This morning you close your eyes to listen. You see Yamamba Girl fall from her shoes. All day she stays with you.

It's no wonder, you think.

We accessorize with skyscrapers, purses the size of bank buildings, ties wide as Interstate highways.

We wear architectural hats and engineered facades.

Imagine two towers— two black stiletto pumps snapped off in the Bay.

A giant girl falls out over the city.

Yamamba falls from her shoes. And we build bridges from her bones.

EXCITING NEW

PRODUCT ANNOUNCEMENTS FROM

JUMBO HENRY, INC.[1]

---

[1] The enclosed product descriptions cannot be authenticated. They have been submitted to you by a whistle-blowing insider who wishes to remain anonymous. When contacted and provided copies of the manuscript, Jumbo Henry, Inc. issued the following statement: "We have good reason to believe these product descriptions and footnotes were penned clandestinely (perhaps illegitimately) by mutinous interns and released to the public in a deliberate attempt to smear the good name of Jumbo Henry Inc.." Said products would have been released in time for Christmas to meet customer demand had Jumbo Henry, Inc. not been investigated by the SEC, BBB, FDA, and FBI. We have confirmed that portions of this transcript has been lifted verbatim from the three-act melodrama "Enron Ain't Got Nothing on Us," performed (until recently) in the Jumbo Henry Towers sixth floor break room every Wednesday at 5:15 under the guise of "Professional Development."

The _____ exercises your child's body and mind. Age-appropriate toys hold baby's interest. Helps achieve developmental milestones. Baby can rock, bounce, spin, stand or sit.[2]

ADULT-SIZED CLASSIC TOYS FOR THE BIG KID IN ALL OF US[3]

The Jumbo Henry Hippety-Hoppety Ball ($89): Reinforced red dimple rubber with Sure-Grip handle and saddle pads. Mounting cleats attached to sides for easy mounting. Hippety-Hoppety has been pressure-tested to accommodate up to 350 lbs. and approx.

---

[2] From product specifications for the Evenflo Exersaucer Deluxe.

[3] This slogan was, of course, created by Jumbo Henry himself and represents perhaps the last significant contribution he made to the company bearing his name before descending into the madness of a world where he believes that boxer shorts are a tool of the oppressive alien colonists and fish-sticks provide all the nutrients any worker could possibly need to survive. It remains a miracle of modern capitalism that the products bearing his name have been so wildly successful and profitable— yet another reason why many ask the questions, crazy or brilliant? Ah, that is a good one.

1500 lbs. of blunt force bounce-pressure. Comes in colors: Elephant Gray, Heather Gray, Kickball Red, and Lime Green. Bounce capabilities equivalent to (if not greater) than Original Hippety-Hoppety Ball[4]. Comes with Jumbo Henry Daypack and Special Hippety Hoppety Expedition Gear. Includes water bottles, signal mirror, real-beef pemmican, reflective tape, golden raisins, pepper spray, and a nylon patch kit. WARNING: Fun of the Jumbo Henry variety can be hazardous to your health.

The La-Z-Boy Recline-O-Saucer (Deluxe Edition, $349): Comes in high-density Stellar Black, Midnight Blue, or Lime Green plastic. Recline-O-Saucer equipped with two drink-holders and a hidden ashtray; mounting brackets and ports for laptop computer with accessories (i.e. DVD, MP3, printer or scanner); food/TV tray; cellular phone storage; waste disposal receptacle[5]; universal remote control and magazine/book rack. Suspension columns employ

---

[4] Jumbo Henry wants you to feel like a kid again. Bounce on a cushion of air and rubber. Jumbo Henry wants you to pretend you're a Kangaroo. Bounce to school. Bounce to work. Bounce to the theatre. Bounce your way to better health. Jumbo Henry wants to facilitate easy mounting. Jumbo Henry likes to imagine himself bouncing to work, around the mall, through the grocery store; and he tells us all about his dreams— making this byoom-byoom-byoom noise and holding his hands out front like he's gripping a saddlehorn. Sometimes he whips the ball with his belt and hollers "YEEHAW" in the office hallways. We couldn't get him off the Hippety-Hoppety prototype. Jumbo Henry wants you to enjoy life. Jumbo Henry wants you to have as much fun as he does.

[5] The Recline-O-Saucer prototype included (thanks to Jumbo Henry's insistence) a portable chemical toilet; but focus groups reacted unfavorably, finding it rather repulsive, and the Porto-Toilet feature was pulled from the final production line.

luxury-car-quality Bilstein Gas Pressure Shock Absorbers. All parts pressure-tested to accommodate 350 lbs. and 3,000 lbs. of leg-torque. Harness constructed of rip-stop nylon with hypoallergenic crotch padding and Comfort-Touch webbing. Rounded base for Wobble Action also includes wobble-stop kickstands with suction pads[6].

Stress Releasing Chew Turtle ($6.99): Made of high-density, non-toxic silicone rubber, the Chew Turtle fits neatly in the palm of your hand, backpack, or purse. Feet and head are ridged, bumped, and scaled for multitude of chew-textures. Shell is harder plastic, good for plaque removal and gum massage. Comes in bright orange with lime green feet and head, or lime green with bright orange feet and head. Rubber bladder belly can be filled with hot or cool water for soothing neck massage[7].

---

[6] Relax while you passively exercise your quads, gluts, and calves. Easy on the knees. Great for circulation. Use on the deck, in the backyard, even at the office. Jumbo Henry knows you want convenience. Convenience and crotch padding. Jumbo Henry believes everyone deserves a harness with hypoallergenic crotch padding. Jumbo Henry also believes everyone wants to sit in our saucer wearing nothing but a tight pair of Teenage Mutant Ninja Turtles underpants. Jumbo Henry thinks every office should make Friday "Diaper Day" and let the custodians go home early. Jumbo Henry does not speak for everyone at Jumbo Henry, Incorporated.

[7] Jumbo Henry wants to "help gnaw your nerves into serenity and masticate your mental anguish into submission." Jumbo Henry believes in the value of a stress-free workplace. Jumbo Henry will understand if you want to chew the imagined head of your possibly insane, potentially genius boss. Jumbo Henry himself "chomps on the surrogate feet of the world's collective angst." He suggests that maybe you too can maw on your deeply ingrained desire to relive the innocent play of your childhood.

Big Daddy Sit-and-Spin ($89): Using revolutionary La-Z-Susan[8] technology and kinetic energy generators, Big Daddy spins just like the Original Sit-and-Spin. Comes in high-density Electric Blue and Lime Green plastic; or in Special Custom Editions: Eric Estrada Highway Patrol, Terminator Steel, Easy Rider Replica, or Low-Rider Chrome with Alien Blue Ground Effect Lighting. 30-inch base fits through most doorways. 14 lbs. plastic, 26 lbs. chrome[9].

Jumbo Giant Brand Whiff-O-Ball Bat and Ball ($12.99): Made from high-density molded plastic, the Jumbo Giant Bat is acoustically engineered to audibly BOOM with every home run thump and line drive dinger. Comes in colors: Fire Engine Red, Pudding White, and Lime Green. Handle heat molded with Sure-Grip Finger Grooves. Equipped with internal glow light for nighttime batting fun. Body textured with "Tru-Wud" Wood Grain. Athlete tested and approved by former major-league baseball player, Fred McGriff. Scientifically weighted for maximum loft and distance. Comes with

---

[8] It is rumored that La-Z-Boy was spawned during a drunken tryst between the late socialite and kitchen cabinet magnet, La-Z-Susan and former TV Personality Mr. Green Jeans after several umbrella drinks at the Toga Lounge in Reno, 1952.

[9] Jumbo Henry wants you to feel like a winner in the Big Daddy Sit and Spinner. Jumbo Henry wants you to zoom-zoom all over the room. Jumbo Henry zoom-zooms a lot, and there doesn't seem to be much we can do about it. And despite boldly printed warnings, Jumbo Henry often stands and walks after using Big Daddy. Last week, Jumbo Henry was so dizzy he fell over a chair in the conference room and broke a rib— a rib from which he suggested we extract the essence necessary to create a Jumbo Henrietta. Though he disputes this, we have checked the minutes and find record that he not only "suggested" but "demanded" that we devote previously allocated resources into a special "Henrietta Project."

one Official Whiff-O-Ball and authentic Fred McGriff Pleather Batting Glove[10].

✑

---

[10] Got some friends? Got some time? Got a white plastic ball with holes? Just add the Jumbo Henry Whiff-O-Ball Bat and you've got a game, friend! A Jumbo Henry staff favorite. Sometimes we shut off the lights in Jumbo Henry Tower, light up the glowing red bat, and Jumbo Henry stands by the copy machine swinging something that looks like an overweight light-saber as we pitch tape balls at him from all angles. Jumbo Henry hits a lot of home runs over the reception desk. Jumbo Henry took the interns to Chuck-E-Cheese's for the Christmas party. He handed out dozens of the Whiff-O-Bat and Ball to parents, danced on stage with the robots, and belly flopped into the plastic balls. He almost killed a kid in a competing party hat and they kicked us all out. For a Holiday Bonus, Jumbo Henry took us to the Flamingo and got himself arrested for stripping down to his TMNT underpants and spanking an exotic dancer onstage. It was the best Christmas party we ever had; and it didn't really seem to matter that we would show up to work the next day and find Jumbo Henry Tower padlocked and swarming with alphabet-named investigative agencies. We learned a lot about business from Jumbo Henry in those days.

AESTHETICS

LIVING WITH A

SPIKE

IN YOUR

BRAIN

A long metal pin from a rototiller flew into his skull and lodged itself in his brain when the man was helping a friend move the machine.

Today, he is still around to tell the story[1].

If he went forward, the pin would move forward. If he would lay down, the pin would sink down.

He says the blunt end of the large pin shot in through his nose. The pin went right past his eye socket, and lodged in the back of his brain.

She says, "He said you need to sit down. He said ____ has a metal pin in his brain. My knees buckled, and I just hit the floor."[2]

J
ones, a probationary butcher, has a steel spike lodged in his brain. You could say it was a memorable accident. Or an accident of memory. Either way he can't get past the picture. There is blood all over the floor. And this eternal watching doesn't bode well for his

---

[1] From "Man Survives Spike Through Head," at http://www.wciv.com/news/stories/0708/534174.html

[2] From "Metal Spike Shoots into Teens Brain" at http://www.koaa.com/aaaa_top_stories/x471793239/Metal-spike-shoots-into-teens-brain

continued employment at the meat shop.

This thing is lodged. Taken up residence. Housed in his skull. Camped. Parked where he won't forget, where he can't even forget long enough to finish the ground chuck order for the day. This spike is punched into his head— sort of like the red-eyed Washington Monument perforating his cerebral city, all the streets of the basal ganglia rerouted, sent roundabout other monuments of memory. It has changed the way everything looks in his head.

Sure there's the dull lump built for his butcher parents— a knot of tangled nerves, wrapped like a twine ball, and rigid with glimpses of inappropriate knife-use. His toddler hands carving a roasted chicken, Mother watching him jab and slip in silence. Father picking at his teeth with the point, trimming toenails with the blade. He's telling Jones about the importance of hygiene; then she's asking Jones to scrape the dead skin from her soles with a serrated Kitchen King. And let's not forget the vast gap of nerves, the major brain renovation from the missing fingertip he sacrificed to the Cuisinart, or the crevasses linked to infrequent but lasting educational experiences with carcasses. But nothing compares to the reach and sting of his spike. A terrible accident. A child's eyes. And everyone still notices.

Jones wears tall hats that sit awkwardly on his head. Sometimes for a joke he will stand in the corner of the butcher shop with a messy beef-apron hanging from his spike, covering his silly face. When his supervisor asks with concern in her voice, Jones tells her not to worry. He is pretending to be a coat rack.

When Jones curls up to sleep at night in his shag-carpet studio apartment, he straps a pillow to his head with an old belt. And of course showering requires a plastic bag for protection. Tomorrow his mother will call and ask about the job. She will remind Jones that he is a third-generation butcher, descended from a long line of ancient Scottish meat cutters. She'll remind him that he is a man of action. She'll remind him not to leave like his father.

The problem is this: occasionally at work Jones is plagued by persistent and distracting daydreams where he wears an array of normal hats— maybe one of those tight-fitting bicycle hats, or a corduroy cap—something with style that still accommodates his spike. He wears a motorcycle helmet, a Yankees cap, a pork-pie hat, and he carries his spike in his hand for show-and-tell. It's kindergarten. It's timeless. And the spike is just an object— something external to him, something he can hold in his hand and control. Or it's just an image on paper, simple pictures of him wearing a baseball cap at the rodeo, watching a monkey riding a dog— something he can keep at home in a drawer. A steel spike of memory. A corrosive remnant. But it's enough to linger. Dodge City Days. That's what it is. The dust and sweet stink of manure. The pack of nervous sheep— spraypainted with red X's and O's. His mother and father still together— but just barely. Clinging to the edges of each other. But Jones stands before Boot Hill Cemetery with the namesake boots protruding from the earth. His picture taken too with a wooden Indian and his little brother. Jones' mother reaching for his father's hand— and he is pulling away, always pulling away, parking himself on a bench. This is before the cowboys fall. This is just hours before his father leaves the Motel for a beer and doesn't come back. This is before his mother drags him to the rodeo anyway and leaves him in the bleachers.

And later that night— with the big lights still burning and the smell of popcorn lingering in the air— Jones wanders the rodeo grounds, kicking an aluminum can. His mother still hasn't found him. But under the bleachers he discovers a noisy teenage girl filleting her arm, carving into it with inefficient strokes. She uses a bad knife, dull and limp, a blade any self-respecting butcher would throw away. She is wearing pedal pushers and a tube top that matches her eyeliner. Her blood is all over. She says her name is Mary. "Go away," she says. "I don't need your help." So he turns around, kicks his can back into the crowds and never tells a soul. Out in the dirt, pushed on by the waves of applause, the Cowboy Monkey rides a black sheep dog. Smiling in chaps and spurs, waving his hat to the crowd, he gallops across the Kansas dirt— that fancy monkey still bouncing back-and-forth through the boy's lonely brain.

HOW NOT TO TELL

A STORY ABOUT

BLOOD

IN A BATHTUB

AN ESSAY ON FORM

"In the final analysis, real suspense comes with moral dilemma and the courage to make and act upon choices."

- John Gardner, "The Art of Fiction."

Do Not:

Say, "You're gonna love this." You're setting yourself up for failure, beginning this way. Don't rush it. Don't go... so there were like bloody chunks of flesh in this bathtub you were supposed to fix, but you were like no way and cursing, and then like out of nowhere this guy shows up, the guy who's staying at the condominium, and he's wearing this cardigan sweater, and that's all you remember of him for some reason— this cardigan sweater, yellow you think, and he's just standing there smiling, and you're thinking he's gonna kill you or something, like Mr. Rogers out for blood, just beating you senseless with his brown shoe or a crowbar or one of those screeching puppets from his show, and like draping your body

with his sweater (a cardigan-wrapped corpse), and then...
Breathe.

Do Not:

Tell us about Stinky, your insipid supervisor, and the way
he peels his eyes at you when you tell him about the call last
night on the emergency line. Don't spend pages and pages
describing his chronic halitosis or the various nicknames—
Ass Mouth, Stink Face, Dragon Breath— or about that
time you tried some sort of pathetic intervention involving
a long discussion about the joys and benefits of tooth-
brushing. Skip all of that. Just tell us what you told Stinky
the morning after, those menacing statements about how
you had, in fact, shut the door on a bathtub covered in
blood, drove home, and went back to sleep next to the
mammal-warm body of your girlfriend. This is enough. It
raises exactly the sorts of questions you want your reader to
ask. Don't feign disinterest in ambulances and sirens and
phone calls from guys in uniforms. These provide important
texture. Because you want your readers to think we know
what happened. Start with the phone call, the voice, the
call for help... You want to set these expectations. You want
to leave us wondering about the man in that ubiquitous
cardigan sweater, his soft voice— like the whisper of...

Do Not:

Start with the blood. Build up to this. Begin with the hard scrape of snow-shovels on concrete walkways. Begin with tourists' toilets— running, clogged, overflowing, flat-busted, refrigerators clanking, water heaters mysteriously unable to provide the endless supply of hot water that a family of six demands. You don't need to waste time with the mundane details of the job, the hours you spend delivering and collecting towels or the times you've fallen asleep in units where you were supposed to fix a closet door and instead sat down to watch basketball or Jerry Springer. None of this is important. Begin with a cell-phone call, ten-thirty at night, the high-pitched ring, and you are thinking, anything but this. Begin (formally) with John Gardner (the pompous ass) and all that crap about real suspense (but aren't we all interested in false suspense?) being the anguish of moral choice (damnit if he's not right, even in an essay like this). Move on to the voice at the other end of the line, maybe the man in the cardigan sweater. We've got blood in our bathtub and, well geez, it won't go down. What would you do?

Do Not:

Repeat blood in the bathtub, blood in the bathtub. The refrain begins to sound like a U2 song or Midnight Oil or the words of some other band with interesting accents and a video. Blood in the bathtub and the world stops turning. This is not a mantra we need any longer. Or perhaps it's *Psycho* we see— the slumping figure of Janet Leigh and the pop-pop-pop of the shower curtain pulling loose, her eye-open face pressed against the tile floor. Either way it yanks us out of the story— you know the one about the man and the yellow...

Do Not:

Mention irrelevant information, such as the name of your favorite breakfast place (The Blue Moose) or how much you like DeWalt power tools, or the innumerable benefits of Sorel muck-luck boots; or mention the stinging joy of first-chair in the morning, before all the tourists wake— the hard crunch of the vinyl pads, still caked with fresh snow; or the early morning silence on the mountain and your envy for first tracks through a field of knee-deep powder, the actual feeling of floating on champagne snow. Sometimes there will be spontaneous whooping. But none of this has any bearing on the story.

Do Not:

Characterize the man in the cardigan sweater as some kind of menace— making not so subtle references to his similarity in size and presence to Marlon Brando (either from *The Godfather* or *Apocalypse Now*). You play with our expectations this way— as if the hapless maintenance man has unwittingly stumbled into the twisted plot of a gang-style execution. We're going to see this coming. We're not going to believe this. We'll recognize the narrator's heavy hand, the overt foreshadowing, and the repeated mention of that yellow cardigan sweater (just the absurdity of it makes it seem menacing, right?). We're going to see him for what he is— a construct, a conceit, a prop for your tale.

Do Not:

Characterize yourself as some sort of Mr. Fix-it Messiah, someone suffering for the sins of all vacationers the healer of toilets, the stopper of leaks, the builder of fires (even if one guy from Florida did pay you twenty dollars to work your fire magic); or try to elevate yourself above your situation. Be honest. You muddy up the waters unnecessarily with talk of delayed dreams and a community culture centered on the snow report and televised cartoons about foul-mouthed eight-year-olds. Leave out mention the cost of a gallon of milk, how much you pay for rent. All of this feels like an attempt to make it seem like there's more at stake for you than there really is.

Do Not:

End with blood in the bathtub. Not that image. Not the slivers of flesh like little fish caught in the drain. Not the knit of a cardigan sweater or a saffron color of yellow— so lewd in this picture.

Do Not:

Tell us the truth about the soft tissue of the esophagus, tears in the wall, holes, and the stomach full of blood. Because you have no idea how someone tears a hole in his esophagus. This is not something you can explain. Do not tell us unless it's to mention that strange feeling you had when Stinky told you the truth— standing in the maintenance office, surrounded by mounds of towels and sheets and tools. A swirl of relief and deep disappointment, as you watched your story gather up it's tangents, sprout wings, and flap out the window— ducking first below your sight line, then rising up and just clearing the tops of the lodge-pole pines before spreading its words and drifting over the valley. Dissipated. Diffused. Gone.

ℒ

COWBOYS
&
INDIAN
DODGE CITY, 1976

Our Old Cigar Store Indians are, without a doubt, the best and most lifelike available, on a limited basis, anywhere... When we engage a master carver to carve a wooden Indian, we discuss the color, look, feel, emotion and design; everything else is in the mind of the master carver, his hands and the log upon which he sits[1].

A photograph: the Wooden Indian's hand smothers the boy's crotch. But he doesn't mind. He sits on a clapboard porch and he clings to the Indian's arm like a baby monkey. The man wears a stiff shirt, his wooden knees shining in the light, denim jeans like the boy. He just sits there with his long black braids, his beaded headband, and one feather rising up in the back. The corners of his mouth are pulled into a frown, his eyes rolled up to the sky. One foot tucked behind the other, he leans toward the boy. He seems to need the boy as much as the boy needs him. His long bony hand, black in the photo, cups the boy's crotch, and his silver ring sparkles against the dark pants. The boy's brother sits on the other

[1] From www.oldcigarindian.com

side of him, still very much alive, holding the Indian's other hand delicately in his own— as if he is visiting the man for tea, sitting with him during the long hours of old age. The brother's white cowboy hat sits in his lap (of course it's white). His short legs barely hang over the edge of the chair. Only eighteen months younger than the boy, he is half the boy's size. He stares at the boy, not at the camera. T-shirt tucked into a big leather belt, the boy mugs his ugly smile for the camera. One brown tooth right in the middle— a mark from a brick. His cheek scar should be there, too, but it's hard to find. He is the Black Hat one. After this, the brothers will ride— outlaws looting barrels of rock candy, swinging cork pistols, and losing at high-stakes games of Go Fish or Crazy Eights. At the cemetery, they will stand over a grave marked with boots toed up through the soil, and each of them will try to imagine what's connected to the feet. Are those the digits of a hanged man, blue with blood and swollen in their socks? They will imagine gun battles and dramatic deaths in the dusty streets. They will imagine their own trigger fingers. But neither of them will imagine that fourteen years later one of them would be standing over the grave of the other. In the photo, the brother's feet are the only feet you can see, and this somehow makes him more real than anything. He's complete, captured for posterity. The Indian and the boy, the chairs, all seem to hover at the edges of the frame. They barely exist the way the brother does. The boy remembers this day. He doesn't remember tumbleweeds or the reflection of parents in a window, something that might make this more of a story. But what remains is not meaning, not some fixed image of brothers, but pure possibility. If they had been outlaw siblings in the Old West, he knows they'd have made friends with this Indian. They might have been a crime-fighting trio. He looks now like petrified wood, as if he was dug out of the desert, dusted off, and propped up on this porch. But he could've still been the boy's friend, even in his wooden state. The brother and he would share. The Indian could've sat in the corner of the boy's room and scared away the dark. The boy would paint and varnish him when he needed it. He'd change his clothes and take him to school. They would be famous together. People would say, "There goes that boy and his wooden Indian." And nobody would whisper about the way he touches him still in this picture.

⠧

THE

PEACH PIT

RODEO

HALF-TIME SHOW

IMAGE 2

TEMPORARILY OUT OF ORDER[1]

---

[1] Due to unforeseen circumstances, this image is temporarily out of order. The Editors regret this inconvenience and assure readers that you will be informed as soon as the situation improves. The image, while clearly exceptional, is simply not here. It should be here, on the page in full color, but it is temporarily certainly not here in working order. The Editors hope there will be a small caption revealing the artist and medium of the work, perhaps some kind of narrative. However, this image, while impressive, is temporarily out of order due to unforeseen circumstances involving weather and insects, and we cannot make any guarantees. The narrative is missing. It shouldn't be here at all. Perhaps at the beginning, but that would change the story, don't you think? It should have been last, as a kind of coda for the show. It could've been lit from below, casting smoky shadows, as if everything in that frame was tight and white and beautiful. The Editors are proud to feature this image and regret the unforeseen spiders that have temporarily rendered this chapter out of order. Some might say chaotic or confusing. Some might say, "Can we go home?" That's not to mention the rain. The Editors assure you that this is not our intention. If things had gone as the writer planned, this image would be in perfect working order and not temporarily compromised due to unforeseen hair and wind and the way a red scarf catches and blows out behind like the flaming burst of a rocket ship. It really should be here, following the spike in the brain, or

maybe scandalously close to the peacock. People would whisper. But this chapter is temporarily, or temporally, out of order. Things don't line up. The timing is all off. If you listen closely you can hear the missing beats. The cuffs don't match the collars. There is no narrative reaching back into history, connecting this chapter with the order of influence. The shit does not hit the fan, but instead gets hung up on the plastic safety screen. The writer has not finished. Due to unforeseen intrusions, possibly involving shiny objects or the scent of lemon rind, this image is temporarily out of line, completely inappropriate. We think it might have been the bent butcher knife. The Editors cannot agree. The Editors do not approve of such images, in so far as we do not endorse the use of coarse language and scatological humor. We also do not endorse nor expressly forbid knives. However, the Editors are proud to house the work of this fine writer and regret that this image, while impressive, is temporarily out of order and is not predicted to be in order anytime soon. The observant reader will notice, however, the complete, if not temporary, absence of visible spiders. This is something we're proud of here. We assure you— and this means something because we own the press— that if this image were not temporarily out of order, you would see, etched into a peach-pit, intricately carved images of a cowboy monkey riding a sheepdog, and you would be moved and touched deeply by this artist's work. You might even offer to purchase the book— simply for the image alone. You wouldn't think about how the artist managed to recreate the little rhinestone-studded vest and the red cowboy hat the monkey was wearing. You'd forget how he captured perfectly the look of horror on the monkey's face, his furry legs strapped to a tiny saddle, as the dog frantically herded four tired sheep into a pen; and you would leave here tonight talking about that one image, the one that should have been over there, scandalously close to the peacock, and how it made you tingle inside.

𝒹𝓅

DEAR ABE

Sometimes he would write with a piece of charcoal or the paint of a burnt stick on the fence or floor. We got a little paper at the country town, and I made some ink out of blackberry briar-root and a little copperas in it. It was black, but the copperas ate the paper after a while. I made Abe's first pen out of a turkey-buzzard feather. We had no geese them days. After he learned to write his name he was scrawlin' it everywhere. Sometimes he would write it in the white sand down by the crick bank and leave it there till the waves would blot it out.

–Dennis Hanks[1]

Abe Lincoln, I've tried writing with coal on a steel shovel, too. I held the black chunk in my hand, my fingers sooty and cramped, pressing it to the tool I dragged in from the garage. This was during one of those times when Mom had to leave, just to get away. This was before the rodeo days, the cowboy, the monkey, and the girl. This was before the smashing chairs. And there was Dad,

[1] From "Abraham Lincoln, the Early Days," at http://www.squidoo.com/abrahamlincolin in a quote attributed to Lincoln's maternal uncle, Dennis Hanks, who claims to have taught Lincoln how to read and write after Abe's mother died.

passed out again, after working all day with the big grey machines. I propped his garden shovel up next to the fireplace and started writing my name; but the coal came apart in my hands, crumbled down to dust, and powdered the beige carpet. Maybe you had better wood to write. Maybe you had nineteenth-century trees. Maybe you had deciduous trees— not the odd geriatric limbs of a few blue spruce dragged in from the yard, not some clumps I claimed from the fire of my parents' fights. I see you stumping for votes. I see your long lanky frame loping down a rutted country road. Alone like me. You pick one track and stay in the dirt path. It's that simple. The roof of your sod house sprouts wild grasses and a small patch of buttercup— their sweet smell hanging in the air. There are no red and blue pollution days. There is no haze of smoke that floats around the breakfast table— a mixture of bacon grease and Kool Menthol in the morning. There is no garage where your father can hide. At night, Abe, you read from borrowed books and practice words on your shovel, the room just barely lit with an oil lamp. You curl up on a cornhusk mattress, cover yourself with goose-down and wool. It's cold in Illinois, cold in this place, too. No wonder you have those sunken windows, those black craters in your face. Your cheekbones like shelves, nose and chin stiff as wooden frames. You have eyes like Dad's. When his shovel crumbles my coal to dust, I paint my eyes like yours— black around the edges. I smear dark shadows on my cheeks. I follow in your footsteps. In this game, the Invisible Mary Todd and me, we go to Ford's Theatre— the two of us propped up in front of the show. We make a good couple.

I hold a paper stovepipe hat in my lap, something I made with scissors and tape. Mother Mary wears a long black dress and she's all stitched up underneath, buckled into her corset. Her posture always perfect. She claps her hands together lightly, three fingers to a palm, and occasionally casts loving glances in my direction. We enjoy the story, the suspense and the comedy. I whisper to her about the stage presence of one actor— a young man with the look of a star. For the first time in a long time, I relax, just lose myself in the story, forget about the war. It's a civil war I try to ignore, the two halves divided, the irrevocable split, the alienation of the other half, the disappearance of everything I've come to depend on. Mary rests her hand on my knee, and lightly fingers my seams. We appear so happy, the two of us together. But something is not right. Slowly my inside arm, my other side, sneaks up behind our chairs and presses the plastic nose of a cap-pistol to the base of my skull. It happens that fast. Pop goes the gun, synchronized with a stage shot. Mary Todd screams. The show ends. Curtain call. My head slumps forward into her lap and my thin Kool-Aid blood pools up in the folds of her dress, runs down the creases into dark spots on the floor, leaving deep rich stains in the beige carpet. Now things are really a mess. The Booth in me, the dramatic side, climbs up on the fireplace hearth and leaps down to the stage, my moonboot tangling in an American flag on the way down. Ignoring the crumpled bones in my ankle, I stumble to center-stage and scream "SIC SEMPER TYRANNUS," then duck behind Dad's La-Z-boy recliner, disappearing offstage. It's a grand exit. But when I look up, Dad stands there, arms dangling around his torso like twigs—those same sunken eyes as you, Abe. It's a genetic thing, he says. I have awakened him, stirred him from his nap, and now he holds my homemade hat in those heavy factory hands. Picked it up from the floor. He doesn't understand, and I can't explain the carpet stains, the coal smears, the pageantry— anything to escape this house. Invisible Mary Todd is nowhere to be seen, just my absent mother's best dress slumped in a chair. Is that my shovel? What in God's name are you doing? Dear Abe, his eyes are all over the soiled carpet, all over my ashen face. His eyes are leaking, seeping water from those dark holes. His eyes are slowly crushing my black paper hat. And I know that the play is finished.

A

LETTER

TO THE

BIONIC MAN

Gentlemen, we can rebuild him. We have the technology...
We can make him better. Better, stronger, faster...

–Oscar Goldman, OSI Director

Steve Austin, who stitched your orange jumpsuit with patches? As a boy I wanted some, too— those embroidered badges of courage and health. I wanted to hear the whisper of doctors: We can rebuild him. We have the technology. Dad used to say my knees were baseballs bulging out. And I've seen you powder a baseball with your fist, crush it down to dust until the leather sloughs off like blistered skin. I bet you could've done the same to my sick limbs.

I've witnessed your recovery from a rolling, flaming wreck— your airplane ripped up on the tarmac and your pained TV voice, "She's breaking up, she's breaking up." They plumbed your astronaut limbs with steel, wired your veins, gave you circuits for nerves. We can make him better, stronger, faster. I needed robotic bones, too. In Mrs. Ricket's class, a virus grabbed my legs, shot pain through my shins. I crumpled in front of the classroom sink. My face broke out with fever blisters, my sinuses clogged with infection. Doctor Pete gave me antibiotics, but I was confused because I thought he gave me *antibionics*, and I knew I didn't want these. But you, Steve Austin, you never suffered from fever dreams like me. You never boiled at one-hundred-and-five, went limp in your mother's arms. You leap over chain-link fences and oncoming traffic. You pulse with a beeping sound— like the electronic drum of a heart. Your bionic eye never misses danger on the horizon.

Steve Austin, I know you make love to a bionic woman who owns a bionic German Shepherd. I've seen the two of you together in the park. She crushes tennis balls with her fist, jumps fences, and pulses just for you. With her one robotic ear, she hears clearly the whispered plots of criminals, the stealthy approach of enemies, oncoming trains— all with bionic drum and cochlea. Maybe the two of you live together in a bionic suburbia. And at night, when robotic Bigfoot has returned to the hills, when the prime-time criminals are sleeping, the two of you sit by a fire oiling your parts. Maybe you talk about the curse of super-senses, the problem with bionic R.E.M. Can your parts keep up with your brain? Can they pulse fast enough? I imagine you must wear an eyepatch to sleep— the thin skin of your eyelid nearly transparent to your robotic pupil.

And I'm sorry for your insomnia. I'm sorry for the pain of bone screws. But at least your bionic mate is there by your side, stitching patches to your suit. She shares your pain and discomfort. She must compensate for technology. Maybe she packs her ear with foam at night, switches it off somehow. I hate to think what she hears— neighbors brushing their teeth, the dilation of your bionic eye, the spawn of mosquitoes in the creek out back. They pop like corn in the night. And maybe she hears me, too, with my baseball knees, my sickened head full of fevers. Because I am still there on the swing-set you built for show. I pump my hips on the rocker-swing until the squeaking brings you to the window. The two of you stand there— you with your eyepatch and she with her ear full of cotton. You might wrap your arm around her shoulder, kiss her wet cheek. You might whisper soft words in her normal ear— because I look very much like the bionic baby you'll never have.

⊘

SMASHING CHAIRS

A REFRAIN

The store's pristine white shelves are filled with china just waiting to be broken.

"I picked pretty things because people are coming in here to do something they aren't supposed to do," Lavely says. "And breaking stuff like this is a little taboo."

The smashing is done in special soundproofed "break rooms" where customers— outfitted in coveralls, boots, gloves and a helmet— stand behind a chest-high barrier and hurl breakables at a stainless steel-covered wall.[1]

What I want to know is: are they going to engage the audience in a cathartic smashing of the barriers of modern discourse? [2]

1

Last Saturday Pop drove the pickup to the flea markets in Serenity and bought himself seven old wooden chairs. Smashing chairs, he called them. Ma says he's doing this 'cause he needs to learn

---

[1] From "Frustrated? Go Break Things at the Smash Shack" at http:// money.cnn.com/2008/09/17/smallbusiness/smash_shack.smb/index. htm?postversion=2008092510

[2] From a google search for "cathartic smashing."

how to control his demons. She holds the boy's chin in her hand and says, "Your father needs an outlet." Then she points at a teapot that just happens to be whistling. It's Friday night, and this is how the weekend begins in their family now that Dad's home again. He's out in the detached garage, cursing and smashing some chairs, splintering them all over the slab floor. Something set him off today, but it's hard to say what it might be. Work? Traffic? Missing keys? The boy couldn't be sure anymore. Sitting on the back porch, he hears the crack-crack of breaking cane. And he doesn't much like the sound of it from there. But he knows when Pop comes out he'll have a smile on his face.

2

Last Saturday Pop drove the pickup to the flea markets in Serenity and bought himself seven old wooden chairs. Smashing chairs, he called them; and he kind of said this with a British accent and a bit of a lisp, drawing out the word "smaaashing." So it's Saturday and he's wearing yellow spandex shorts around the house. This morning, before the boy awoke, Pop drove to the all-night hardware store, bought sheets of sandpaper and some blue suede work gloves. At breakfast he talked about buying a Chihuahua and naming it Charles. Now he's cleared space in the detached garage for the six chairs he has left and spread cardboard over the slab floor. Ma says he's doing this 'cause he needs an outlet. The boy sees electrical, thinks electrocuted; but she means artistic. Ma holds the boy's chin in her hand and says, "You have to understand." Then she chomps down on her pinky fingernail and spits the sliver on the kitchen floor. The boy sweeps it up quickly with the potato shavings and dumps it out back. Pop's out there now in the garage again, probably sanding and varnishing old wood. He's customizing the spindles with pastel colors and singing show tunes. He's expressing himself, and the boy doesn't much like the sound of it coming in through the back door. But he knows when Pop comes back he'll have a smile on his face.

3

Last Saturday Pop drove the pickup to the flea markets in Serenity and bought himself seven old wooden chairs. Smashing chairs, he called them. Ma says he's doing this 'cause he needs to learn how to express his love. She says he needs an outlet. The boy sees water released from a dam, and she means he's flooded. She holds the boy's chin in her hand and says, "You have your father's teeth." So here they are in the backyard on a Saturday afternoon, father and son wearing motorcycle helmets and body armor made out of street signs. Each of them holds a sheet metal sword and a smashing chair. They dance around the yard, jabbing and blocking with their chairs, swinging wildly with their heavy swords. Pop smacks the boy good with a chop to the head, and he catches his father with a glancing shot to the ribs. Pop bends over. The boy walks toward him, and he lunges, thrusting for the boy's torso with his chair. The boy swings down hard with his chair, catches his father on the back of the head, and sends him face first into the ground. He's out cold for a few seconds, prostrate in the mud. He wakes up woozy, speaking in tongues. And the boy doesn't much like the sound of it. But he knows when Pop wakes up he'll have a smile on his face.

4

Last Saturday Pop drove the pickup to the flea markets in Serenity and bought himself seven old wooden chairs. Smashing chairs, he called them. And now he plans to sell them door-to-door all over the upper Midwest. Therapeutic antiques, he calls them. Ma says he's doing this 'cause he needs to be needed. The boy thinks parasite, but she holds the boy's chin in her hand and says, "That's not fair." How does she know? At dinner Pop tells them how he'll drive a camper truck, hit garage and estate sales, and buy all the flimsy Smashing Chairs he can find. He'll fix them up, turn around, and sell them right back. A tidy profit, too. So out in the garage tonight, he practices his sales pitch. *The Housewife's Friend. Don't let that Grumpy Bear take his frustration out on you. Buy him the Smashing Chair! And watch your marriage problems melt away.* He'll also sell them as The Workingman's Answer to Therapy. *Don't let some shrink dope you up! Just Smash a Smashing Chair and feel a new sweetness in the air.* Pop fashions himself some kind of feminist or self-help guru. He wants to help others wrestle with their demons, the boy supposes. On his way to bed, he stops by the boy's room to tell him that the next stop is the Home Shopping Network. And the boy doesn't much like the sound of it from his bed. But he hopes when Pop comes out the other end of this he'll have a smile on his face.

5

That last Saturday Pop drove the pickup to the flea markets to find Serenity, but bought seven old wooden chairs instead. Smashing chairs, he called them. Only six left. Six for our sins, he says, as he lines them up around the tiny table for Sunday dinner. The family crowds in, the old chairs rubbing spindles against their backs, snatching at them with their splinters. Pop hardly eats and just stares at the chairs as if they're his true children. He talks to one of the closer ones in hushed intimate tones, and Ma begins to cry. Pop stands up suddenly, knocking his plate to the floor and dropping silverware like seed. He grabs the chair he's been talking with most, clutches it to his chest and glares at us through its spindles. He pushes past Mother and the other chairs, and stomps out the back door. This last Pop image. The boy sees time stop. And no matter how many ways he repeats and revises this story, it always ends the same. Mother melting at the table. A slam of the door. Pop's in the detached garage again. A few minutes later— the new clatter of cane on the slab floor. Then silence. And he doesn't much like the sound of it from where he stands, his arm around Ma's shoulders, her head resting against his chin. Because he knows without looking that Pop probably won't have a natural smile when he finds him later— his legs swaying above the floor, his body twisting from the rafters, propelled by that one swift kick off his chair. But the garage will fill with a soft rhythmic creaking— almost like the drift of our front-porch swing, but heavier still— and sometimes in the right kind of story the noose has spread his purple lips and given the boy their teeth to remember.

ℒ

POSTCARDS

FROM THE

COLD WAR

NOTES ON VIEWING *THE DAY AFTER*

The most important movie we or anyone else ever made[1].

-Brandon Stoddard
President of ABC Motion Pictures, 1983
Referring to *The Day After*

IMAGE/VOICES

September 16. Mr. Hendry takes Mrs. Hendry by the hand. She's calling the kids to the table for a country breakfast. "Just wait a minute," he whispers, tanned muscles rippling beneath stained overalls. "But, honey, the biscuits...," she says, halfheartedly, and follows him anyway. They live

---

[1] The made-for-TV post-apocalyptic drama, *The Day After*, aired on a Sunday in November, 1983. After the bombs dropped on screen, the movie was shown without commercial interruption. It earned the second highest ever Nielsen Rating for a TV movie, trailing only *Gone With the Wind*. President Ronald Reagan noted in his journal that after viewing the movie that he felt "greatly depressed," and the director, Nicholas Meyer believes that the movie helped change Reagan's mind about his approach to the Cold War and, therefore, forever altered the course of history. He could be right. Or not.

next door to a missile silo. But she knows what he's after. Sex, of course. Sex distraction. High-pitched warning signal sounds, screeching from the TV box. Children prone before the pictures. Parents smiling as they tiptoe past their children, past the television, upstairs, sly grins across their faces. Guilty. Horny. Guilty. Horny. They ignore the alarm. Parents ignore the alarmed children.

VOICE

Blonde TV newswoman sputters: That's THREE nuclear weapons in the low kiloton range airburst this morning over advancing Soviet troops. She hardly believes what she's saying. She can't sell this story, can't muster courage. Her voice halts and fails, stumbles over the words. Her professional demeanor crumbles on camera. Right there. In front of the boy. This is how it begins.

IMAGE

Soldiers running for trucks. Soldiers running for planes. Soldiers running. The frantic clatter of their boots. The pumping limbs. The thumping.

Up the down ladders. Down the up ladders. Into planes. Into holes. Into this thing too deep now to get out. Too far.

Image/Voices

Sister Hendry tries to pull her brother away from the television, yanking on his arm. "Kenny. Kenny. Come on," she says, voice stretched and urgent. Do I know this boy, Kenny? Was he in my Boy Scout troop, my elementary school, my baseball league? He looks like Karl, the kid from my neighborhood who wears his brother's hand-me-down jeans. Karl with the big belts. Karl with his butt hanging out. Where will the children go? Outside? The cellar? Will she interrupt her parents' lovemaking? Does she understand that this is the apocalypse and they have abandoned them? The bombs are coming. Upstairs. Her parents are fucking.

Image

Pale hands working white-capped levers up and down. Rapid jerking movements. Just hands. No face. Sweaty and urgent. Are we in an airplane?

Is that a fuselage/Missile silo? Bunker? Hard to say for sure. Just pictures of hands. Disembodied hands. All over. Hands all over.

IMAGE

Buttons. Red. White. Voices in the background. Codes entered by hand. Fingered. Punched. Numbers. Hand scribbling across the paper, putting numbers into boxes. Punching keys. Scratching. Harsh black pencil marks. Just frantic hands. No person. Hands over hands. Here is the church. Here is the steeple. Open the doors. See all the...

MAN'S VOICE/ IMAGE

"Runway 0, 5, 3 6, 1," he says. Hands drifting over switches and dials, adjusting instruments, the piano man's hands making decisions for all of us. Automatic pilot. Automatic violence. Automatic for the people. Finish what has been...

MAN'S VOICE/ IMAGE

Started now. Nuclear bomb of undetermined strength exploded over NATO regional military headquarters. At home Kenny Hendry sits on his knees in front of a large television, glow of screen illuminating his face. He cannot move. He can only gawk at the coming storm. Mouth open. Eyes wide. Hands on his legs. Here he is, late 20th Century Supplicant. Worshipper. See how he looks as if he will be sucked into the news. Looks like we all feel— living in the penumbral blue glow of cathode ray.

IMAGE

Raised to see. Pilot in white helmet speaks into headset microphone. Close-up of his face. Flat, wide, expressionless. Just doing his job. Chattering. Professional discourse. But what is his job now? What is the point? He is obsolete now. Extinct. Soldier dinosaurs. In the air. Down below the surface. Fossilized in their chairs. Radios will fall silent. What's the point in landing? Circle now. Tight at first. Widening out until our pilot drifts beyond the curve of the earth.

IMAGE

Silent Dahlberg boy filling milk jugs with well water watches jet streak across cloud-spattered sky. Pump squeaks. Birds chirp. The red dog lying in the grass. Tiny hand working the pump. Primed. Pushed into the apocalypse.

IMAGE/ VOICES

Radar screens, spinning green line rotates around the axis. Boop. Boop. Sonar blipping. Clusters of incoming warheads. Red buttons. Red buttons. Beeping. Alarms sounding. Cacophony of voices and noise. NINER. NINER. Foxtrot. Charlie. SEVEN. SEVEN.

IMAGE

B52, big-ass bomber lifts off, aching to rise, loaded with ordinance. Goaded for ordinary gifts. Lifts up and over distant hills. Pulls wheels up into its belly. Disappears. There's nothing left. Less the giant black bird floating over the near-dead. Riding thermals. Dropping mushroom seed.

MOMENT

Jim Dahlberg thinks about practical concerns. He carries a box of canned food to the basement cellar. His wife bakes perishable pies, getting ready for the wedding reception tomorrow. Has to feed sixty-seven people. Sixty-seven guests. Welcome to the new world. Their daughters are busy upstairs. Primping, curling, applying. Pretending that everything is the same. Jim struggles to convince his wife that she has other things to worry about, tries to tell her about the bombs. Understatement is therapy in this thing. He says, "We're pretty near under a national emergency here." But Mrs. Dahlberg doesn't want to hear any of this. Not now. Not today. She has a wedding to plan, a perfectly tragic wedding. Joleen enters the picture, appearing from the right. You only see the back of her head. But I know her. I know this girl, Ellen Anthony. She is my age, my time, my missing life. She went to my school, lived in my neighborhood. But now she is just playing a part, reciting her lines. She says, "The man on the television said there was going to be a war and that we should unplug all of our electrical appliances." She asks her parents, "There's not going to be a war is there?" But we already know the answer. We already see the answer. We already see the front. They can't face the truth.

IMAGE

Hands twisting on the nose-cones of missiles. Loading weapons onto planes. Gloating at military might. Yellow and white bodies. Phallic ordinance clutched to white bellies. Men running. Yes, Ellen. Yes, Joleen. Men running. Men dying. Women and children. White horses. This IS the war. This IS the end. Turn off your televisions. This is.

TEXT/ IMAGE

Yellow block letters pasted on the Screen: SAC Airborne Command Post (Over Kansas). Airplane drifts across the sky, still far away. Still too close. Still and silent against a blue immensity. Peaceful almost. Quietly surreal. No rattle and hum. Know this silence will not last. Know it is bright with kinetic violence.

IMAGE/ VOICES

Curly haired man in blue jumpsuit has red neck-
kerchief stuffed into front. "Sir, we need access
to the keys and the authorization documents at
this time." And we know what these keys can do.
We understand how they unlock the future. We
have something invested in this story. The dual
keys. The final safeguard. The hands. The keys.
Clutched between white fingers. Inserted. With a
simultaneous twist. This is how the end begins.

VOICE

OK, do you have your key? It takes two to go. Two
to twist the switch. Two to make another. Two
parents to leave them before the television, news
on, eyes open. Two to neglect the biscuits. Two to
start one of these things. It takes two to war.

IMAGE

Together the men stand and open a large red
metal box. Together they open the box. Together
they remove what's inside. But what IS inside? I

can't see it. I can't see anything. None of it means anything.

VOICES/IMAGES

Red pickup stops on a gravel road. Driver says, "Sorry I can't take you any further." Birds twitter in the trees. Steve Gutenberg waves goodbye and walks down a country road, blue frame backpack slung over his shoulder. He gazes pensively at his surroundings. Cows wander down toward him from a red barn as if they know him. The silence is overwhelming, the quiet at the eye. The pregnant pause. Birth of a disaster. An orange swing set. A field of wheat. Crows cawing. Things are too quiet. We know this already because we understand the narrative. A white horse stands in a green pasture, tail swishing in the air. The proverbial calm. The proverbial white horse. The proverbial Steve Gutenberg. Why is he here, at the center of the frame, fully in focus? We don't know for sure. He left school. Hitchhiked, heading for somewhere near Harrisonville, Missouri. We don't know much. But we know something is about to happen. We can feel it in the silence.

IMAGES

Jerky camera, bounces around, follows men in blue uniforms. The men wear red neck-kerchiefs. Redneck war chiefs bearing down on buttons. One sits at a desk. Others scamper around. Sitting. Standing. Up. Down. Cacophony of voices in the background. I can't decipher any of it, can't read the codes. Perhaps you can see better. The children are missing from the picture. Picture the children missing, the meek inheritance, their meager parents. Picture the parents missing this. Because they cannot see.

VOICES

Disembodied: "Alpha 7 8 November Foxtrot 1 5 5 2." A foreign tongue. Wagging the language of military action. The dogs of war. Woofing in the woods, nipping at the heels of foxes.

VOICE

Soldier in silo: This is Oscar 11. "We just started, sir." But it is already too late. Two little children.

Two brothers. See this stock footage, these training films. Soldiers drilling, practicing the apocalypse. Footage pilfered, procured from government archives. Docu-drama feel. Adding and subtracting from the truth. My brother and I watch, wait, lunging at the bait. The Hendry children play innocently in the grass. Waiting to be overcome. I want to reach out to them, pull them through.

VOICE

Disembodied voice in silo next door: "We gotta get outta here." But where will they go? They don't know where nowhere is anymore. Anywhere but here. In Kansas. Targeted town. Targeted farm. Family or not. Children or none. The bombs are coming. And there's no place like home. No place like home. Three times and maybe you can escape.

VOICE

Step One: Launch keys inserted.

Voice

Disembodied: Belching out NAVAL-SWITCH-
NAVAL. Repeat: NAVAL-SWITCH-NAVAL.
Picking up phone. Keys inserted. Five, Four... A
partial countdown, abbreviated, attenuated. The
suspense of interrupted sequence.

Image

Mother Hendry stands in front of her dresser,
wearing only a towel, brushing her brown hair.
Meditating, wallowing, watching her reflection.
She is glowing from the fucking. The dresser
begins to shake and rattle. She hears the rip and
roar, the noise of their neighbor, the Minuteman.
She runs to the window. Face pressed to the glass.
As a missile bursts from the yard. Has she forgotten
the children altogether? Was it good for her? The
biscuits are already burned.

Images

One after another. The slam of silo doors
opening. The hard fuck. The shuck and jive of

silo machinations. White feathers of steam sprout
from the earth and spit loaded missiles into the
sky. Aiming for a red patch. Shooting for soil.
Head long Russian in your sights.

IMAGES

Blond Hendry boy bathed in the blast. Kenny
and sister standing in the grass. Plastic toys in the
yard. Swing set, too. Mouths spread in identical
exaggerated "O's." I can almost hear the director
saying, "Imagine you see missiles in the air." The
neighbor is noisy for the first time. The silo next
door belches white smoke. The silo next door
roars awake. Father Hendry sits on a tractor,
raising hand over brow, gazing up at the sky. The
white horse bolts and runs. Spooked. Slow motion
gallop, suspended animation, suspended white
innocence.

IMAGE

Mother's face framed in the window, watching the
neighbor erupt. Runs downstairs, "You kids come
in here right now!" She wants them close now,

wants to protect them. But she must know that it's too late. She wants to be a mother, but she must know that it's over. She runs into the yard, past the truck, reaches for their O-shaped faces. This is when the fire takes her, spreading across the screen like a spill. Until all of them are tarred with the flame.

Images

White noise roar and rumble of first strike. Pores of the planet opened up, leaking bombs. Gushing with warheads. Popping their payloads. The screen is filled with an orgy of ordinance. Weapon porn. Apocalyptic snuff. Too much, you think. Too far. But all of it is real. Actual footage. Stock film. Samples of the rapture. And you can't pretend you haven't seen it before.

Image

A man stops painting a wall to watch, brush suspended mid-swipe, bristles pressed against fresh paint. Animated man. Late 20th-Century worker. White pants and everything. You try not to think about your own time with the brush. The daily grind. Mind on anything but war. What a way to go.

IMAGE

Two men working on a satellite dish turn and watch, staring up at the sky. You can see it in their eyes. Over. Their day is done. Melted in a dish. Communication hardware pointless now. This is who we see. These random clips. Mixed in with images of the classroom. The desks, the children. The kids you know. Forget that you see Kendall Meade in the back row. Forget the way he is vaporized...or skeletonized. Flesh melted. Nothing but bones left. Forget the way this image will linger, trapped in the spin of your memory.

IMAGE

Missiles rise over South Park gazebo. Flowers splashed across the foreground. Pools of color. People stand and stare. Point at a blue horizon filled with rising bombs. Gawking at the end we have delivered. Us from evil. Them from good.

The rest of us left looking. Up from below. Toes tingling in our shoes. It doesn't matter if we remember this moment.

IMAGE

Frozen and framed, stamped to your brain. Missiles rise over Douglas County Memorial Hospital. White streaks cutting through blue. Staff in scrubs gathered on the sidewalk. Pointing. Staring. My brother and I were born here, before the end. White daggers streak artificially across the sky. Special effects. Let's all watch, too. Watch and learn. But shield your eyes against the bright blast. Don't stare. Lest hair grow from palms, your face chiseled that way, or maybe you'll suck it down your windpipe. Maybe you'll swallow the thousand suns. Maybe you'll let them stew in your gut. And maybe if you gaze into your navel. Through that window in your belly button. You will see the way this movie nestles in next to your vital organs like unchecked cells. Like a kind of tumor or vehicle to your tenor. Maybe if you see it right. Use a different lens. Maybe then you will understand.

IMAGE

Missiles rise over Memorial Stadium packed with people. Watching football. Home game. A losing effort no doubt. How about we all go home? Forget this. Forget watching the sport of war. Must be Saturday. Must be more than a game. Now a place where your name dies. And the day after would be Sunday. Tomorrow. The day of rest. The first day of the new world. Stepping out from the inexplicable rubble.

IMAGES

Missiles rising. Missiles rising. Rising. RISING. So many missiles rising. A glut of bombs. But still the white horse circles, pushing against the fence. Still Steve Gutenberg walks.

MOMENT

Truckload of soldiers drive up to the silo next door to the Hendry's house. They drive a green truck. Orange light on top. Two white soldiers. One black soldier. We know him from before. We know him from the scene with his wife in Sedalia. She clutched a baby in her arms. She didn't want him to go, didn't want him to leave her and the child. But he is a soldier, and this is his duty. We will remember her when the soldier asks someone later about Sedalia and he says, "There ain't no Sedalia no more." So here he is. Soldiers silly with angst. And the missiles are already in the air, already blooming from the horizon. They know there's nothing more they can do. They sit in the truck. Watching. The white soldiers talk of guarding the silo, doing their job, fulfilling their duty to the president, the country, the future. They work for wasting away. But the black soldier says, "The war is over, man. Can't you see that? The WAR is OVER." His wife and child are dead. There ain't no Sedalia no more. And he is the only one who makes any sense. The war is over and there is nothing now but fallout.

∂ρ